Table of Contents

Leslie
Thompson

CHAPTER ONE
Science, No Fair!

High school is going nowhere near as great as I'd planned. I can't believe I'll be graduating this year and I still haven't kissed a boy. I mean, what the heck is wrong with me? Am I really that lame?

I sigh loudly to myself.

I am.

I stare out of the classroom window and watch the raindrops roll down the glass. No sunlight in sight, only dreary skies and damp landscape.

It's awfully dark to be one in the afternoon. It seems to storm almost every day lately. I hate the start of Spring, it's always so gloomy.

"Hello? Ms. Thompson, earth to Ms. Thompson!" Mr. McClain exclaims in my direction, breaking me out of my self-pitying daydream. The entire class chuckles at my obvious preoccupation. I become instantly embarrassed.

"Present," I mumble, assuming he is taking attendance near the end of class. He shakes his head disappointedly.

"I think we already established that when you got here 45 minutes ago. I was referring to your assignment on the *Great Depression*, but it seems like you're experiencing your own version of a great depression right now." He looks at me from over the top of his glasses and the class laughs louder. I sink down in my chair, feeling smaller than I did before.

The bell rings and I sigh with relief. I'm not good with public humiliation, no matter how dismal or huge the display is. I gather my belongings slowly to allow time for my classmates to rush from the classroom. I stand from my seat after the coast is clear. I place one strap of my navy blue bookbag over my shoulder and head towards the exit. I move swiftly past Mr. McClain's desk.

"I'm sorry, Leslie. I didn't mean to embarrass you. It seemed like something was bothering you and I wanted to make sure you were OK."

I halt in my tracks, even though I'm not too keen on doing so. I produce a fake smile as the words, *"YEAH RIGHT"*, run through my mind repeatedly. If he was really concerned, he would have pulled me to the side after class like a normal teacher.

"Are you OK?" I shake my head yes, still maintaining my phony grin. I really need to get out of here as quickly as I can. One more class and I'm home free. He sighs as if he can tell I'm lying, "OK, but if you need to talk to someone, I want you to know that I'm always here to listen." I nod once more before hurrying away from him. I've never liked Mr. McClain. He's always given me creepy old-man vibes.

I reach the hallway and proceed to my locker. I need to exchange my history materials for my science book before I head to my last class. I'm anxious to get this school day over with. It's Thursday, meaning I'm only one day away from the weekend. I'm overly ready for a break from this teenage asylum. Plus, I'm so looking forward to sleeping in for two whole days.

"Les, what happened to you?" I turn around and spot my best and only friend, Kyra, standing behind me. She swoops her long, pressed hair behind her triple-pierced ear. I sigh once I remember that I was supposed to meet her by the drinking fountain after the last bell.

"I'm sorry, but Mr. McClain was being Mr. McClain again." She shakes her head at my explanation as if she knows exactly what I mean.

"Ugh, acting all creepy and disturbing?" I laugh after she rolls her eyes at the thought of him. She has him the hour before I do.

"No, being publicly offensive and then trying to clear it up privately so we won't tell our parents." She nods as if she can relate. I turn towards my locker to rummage through my belongings, "I had to stop by my locker anyway. I forgot to grab my science book." Kyra smacks her lips.

"I should've forgotten mine. Lugging around this heavy darn book all day has my back hurting." I smile at her after I slam my locker shut. We walk swiftly in the direction of our next class, worrying that the tardy bell is going to echo throughout the halls before we make it. We cross our class's threshold just in time to hear the annoying chime. Our teacher, Mrs. Weaver, gawks at us while we make our way to our chairs positioned next to each other. She clears her throat once we are seated.

"Good afternoon, class. Today is a special day!" She stands up happily, tugging at her too big skirt on her petite frame before she continues, "Today is the day that you find out who your science fair project partners are!"

She speaks excitedly, but the entire class vocally expresses their disapproval. She looks taken aback by the unenthused reaction. She steps in front of her desk, "Come on guys, don't act like this! This is the most rewarding time of the year for the science community! The time when all my brilliant students get to dig into the depths of their imaginations and come up with brilliant ideas and brilliant solutions! The sky's the limit when it comes to science!"

I tune her out to glance at Kyra. Kyra glances at me as well, causing confident smiles to form on both of our faces. We've been science fair project partners for three years running. She and I have an amazing time doing our projects together. We've never gotten anything lower than an "*A*" and we're undefeated at the science fair convention. We look at each other as if we already have this victory in the bag. Beating out our grade, the entire school and then other schools in the district is how our school years typically end. Us bringing home the Science Fair Championship trophy is the one thing we can look forward to every Spring.

It's officially our time to shine.

"So… OK, without any further ado, the science fair partners!" Mrs. Weaver picks up a paper from her desk and glances at it. She looks in me and Kyra's direction immediately, "Umm, one quick thing before I start. It was brought to my attention by the principal that we have a few students in academic trouble. They must pass this class in order to graduate, so they've been paired with students that excel in this class. Please don't get mad if you don't get the partner you want. Those having a hard time deserve a shot at academic glory."

She clears her throat, "Amy, you're with Cynthia." The ladies air high-five each other from across the room. "Larry, you're with Benjamin." They look at each other but don't react to the news. "Kyra, you're with Brandon." Kyra gasps loudly like she can't believe what she just heard. Our mouths hang open when our shocked eyes meet. We both appear stunned by the surprising turn of events. Our sights dart in Brandon's direction, who is always sporting his varsity jacket and backwards fitted cap. A grin appears on his light-skinned face. He nods his head as if he approves.

"Leslie, you're with Marcus." My ears go deaf after Mrs. Weaver's words. My jaw drops lower than it was before. Kyra's eyes burn a hole in the side of my face, but I'm unable to look at her right now. My whole body is paralyzed from the science teacher's devastating news.

I can't believe she just said my partner is Marcus Tate! Please, God, anybody but Marcus Tate!

I glance backwards towards Marcus's seat and notice him smirking in my direction. His girlfriend, Tori, is posted next to him with the evilest expression on her face. I slouch down in my seat when the room closes in on me. I want to have a panic attack right now, but I try hard to keep it together. If I have a full-fledged breakdown in front of the entire class, I will never be able to live it down.

I can't believe the teacher broke me and Kyra up and put me with Marcus Tate! My grade cannot be dependent on how well I'm able to get along with that prick! There must be something I can do about this!

The teacher pairs up the remainder of the class while I stew in devastation. I lay my head on the desk once my headache starts. I close my eyes tightly, briefly recapping the middle school torture I endured from that punk and his loser friends. Ever since we crossed paths in the 6th grade, he's been the bane of my existence. He tormented me, shoved me around, and even locked me in the janitor's closet for an entire school day before. He is the epitome of all things wrong with the opposite sex.

I HATE MARCUS TATE!

"Hey, are you OK?" Kyra touches my arm, distracting me from my traumatizing thoughts. I lift my head and glare at her dark brown face with stress-filled eyes. I don't answer her, but she knows exactly how I feel without me having to say anything. She was there to experience the emotional distress that Marcus caused in the past. She gives me a sympathetic look.

"It's OK. We'll just ask Mrs. Weaver if we can switch. It's no big deal," she whispers to me, causing me to expel the breath I've been holding since Mrs. Weaver's bomb dropped on me. Kyra is always looking out for me, and I love her so much for that.

The class wraps up and we instantly dart to Mrs. Weaver's desk. She looks up at us from her seat as if she already knows what we are about to complain about.

"Sorry ladies, but there's nothing I can do."

"We're not about to ask if we can work together, if that's what you're thinking. I mean, yeah, we're upset about not being partners, but we actually wanted to ask you something else." Mrs. Weaver gives Kyra her undivided attention while she continues, "We were wondering if we could switch partners? It's just that Leslie would work better with Brandon and Marcus, well…" Mrs. Weaver breaks their eye contact as if she's about to deliver more disappointing news.

"I really wish I could ladies, but there's nothing I can do about that, either. The principal is the one that did the pairings. If you want, you can talk to him about switching you guys up. It's really out of my hands." She smiles at us slightly before putting a stack of papers into her work bag. I let out a hopeless sigh, watching my Valedictorian status crumble right before my eyes. Kyra snatches me out of the room and down the emptying hallway.

"Come on," she spits out, continuing to drag me past my locker. I stop her, causing her to gawk at me weirdly.

"Where are we going?" She looks offended by the question.

"Duh! To the principal's office! We need to get this mistake straightened out." I shake my head at her bad idea.

"We can't, and you know why." She makes a confused face before a light bulb appears to go off in her mind. She sighs loudly and leans against the wall.

"Oh yeah… that's right. Marcus is the principal's son."

"Exactly. Remember that time when the whole football team got into that huge brawl during one of their away games? Everyone got suspended except Marcus and a few of his dumb friends. I can think of a dozen more times when Marcus should have flunked, gotten caught after doing something stupid, or been suspended, but it never came to pass. There is nothing Principal Tate won't do to get his privileged son out of trouble."

Kyra nods her head as if she agrees, "Ugh, you're so right, but out of everyone in the class, why did you have to be paired with him? That is so cruel! Everyone knows that you and Marcus don't get along."

"Apparently not everyone," I reply in a defeated tone, leaning my body against the wall as well. "I mean, I do have the best grade point average in our senior class. Statistically speaking, his son will have the best chance at passing science if he's paired with the most academically inclined person in school." I look down and take a deep breath, "I guess it is what it is. I'm not going to let this science fair assignment with Marcus ruin my perfect G.P.A. If I have to work with that jerk, then so be it. I'm looking forward to the day when all this mess is over with."

Marcus
Tate

CHAPTER TWO
PLEASANTLY SURPRISED

I struggle through Friday's school day, thanks to my terrible mood. I'm usually ecstatic on the day before the weekend but knowing that I must work with Marcus very soon has me stressed the heck out.

I make it to science class earlier than everyone, including Kyra. I've been avoiding her all day. I'm not in the mood to talk to anyone right now. I'm more interested in getting through this last hour of school so that I can go home and climb in my bed. Until then, I must keep my mind at ease. I reach in my bag for my art supplies.

Other students arrive while I doodle in my drawing pad. I work on a picture of a girl that resembles me sitting on a rocket ship. She appears to be happy about being on her way to far and distant lands.

Sometimes, I wish I could fly away and never come back.

That's why I love drawing. I can be whoever I want to be and go wherever I want to go. No hangups, insecurities, rules, or judgments to worry about. I'm free to be me unapologetically.

I wish I could be like that in real life.

I'm shading in the girl's curly locs when someone steps in front of my desk. Their presence covers my source of light, slightly irritating me.

"So... I guess you and I will be working together, huh?" I close my eyes and sigh when I hear Marcus's voice. My eyes reluctantly travel up his tall body, "I can't wait." He smirks at me, provoking me to give him an evil glare in return. He makes his way to his assigned seat in the back of the classroom. Kyra walks up and sits in her chair.

"Ugh, what did he want? Are you OK?" She gazes at me with a concerned look after her questioning. I shake my head yes before closing my artbook and stowing it in my bookbag. Mrs. Weaver walks in right after the bell rings.

"Good afternoon, class. Today, you are going to start your projects. I need you to link up with your partners so that you can brainstorm a few ideas and exchange contact information. I want you to communicate over the weekend and decide on a project topic. I expect to hear a finalized decision from each team on Monday." I sigh to myself and close my eyes again, completely dreading any form of at-home communication with Marcus Tate. Kyra turns to say something to me, but Brandon walks up and interrupts her.

"Hey, Kyra. Should we get started?" She glances at his freckled face before looking back at me.

"Are you going to be OK?"

"Yeah," I assure her quickly with a fake grin. She notices my deceit but gets up and stands next to Brandon anyway. She knows I hate pity parties, so she tries not to worry about me too much. I know she does, though. That's just the type of friend she is.

I watch her thick frame walk towards Brandon's seat and notice Marcus walking in my direction. I breathe deeply while trying to stay calm. He parks himself at Kyra's desk and slides it closer to mine. He tries to engage with me, but I turn away from him.

"Hey, Leslie, long time no talk to." I cut my eyes in his direction.

"That's not true. Just last week, you called me an ugly giraffe." He snickers a little with a head shake and I become aggravated. He notices my seriousness and tries to explain himself.

"But that wasn't me, though… that was Tori. You know how she is." I glance back at her light brown face while she sits with her partner, Barry, and her hazel eyes meet mine. I immediately turn away from her.

"Doesn't matter. You might as well have said it; that is your girlfriend." He glances back at her as well before making a bothered expression.

"Yes. Yes, she is."

The mentioning of Tori seems to put a damper on his mood. The quietness that we are suddenly sitting in validates my observation. I want to ask him what's plaguing him, but I really don't care enough to know. Things slowly get awkward between us, causing me to look around uncomfortably. I decide it's time to get down to business.

"So, do you have any ideas for our science fair project?" He looks at me as if he's glad I changed the subject.

"I'm just here to follow your lead and do whatever you need me to do. After all, you are the undefeated champion of the science fair convention." I blush a little at the sound of my greatest achievement leaving his lips, "That's why I requested for you to be my partner."

I look at him surprisedly, feeling flattered that he would want to work with me over everyone else. Then, I remember that I'm the smartest person on paper and my exalted feelings diminish immediately.

"Yeah, a sure win," I spit out sarcastically. He notices my tone and turns his body towards mine.

"That's not what I meant. I mean, I do like winning, which is no secret. I am the captain of an undefeated football team." He toots his own horn and I roll my eyes, "But I also wanted to spend some time with you. You and I have a 'not so good' history, but our future doesn't have to be the same way. I was never the nicest person to you and that's been bothering me lately. I just wanted a chance to apologize and show you that I'm not the same immature little boy I used to be in middle school."

He stares vulnerably in my eyes, which surprises me somewhat. He seems so genuine, which is a trait that Marcus Tate has never possessed before. His sincere tone has me second guessing my hate for him. My guard eases down as we chat a little longer about assignment ideas. He makes a couple of jokes and I laugh.

I can't believe it! Is Marcus Tate making me smile? I never would have guessed it.

"Alright class, wrap it up. It's almost time for the final bell." Mrs. Weaver breaks up my moment with Marcus and I feel slightly disappointed. Things were going surprisingly well between him and I.

"Hey babe, done with *her* yet?"

I spoke too soon.

Marcus and I look up and see Tori's fit body standing in front of us. Everything about her is super intimidating. I awkwardly look down at the pencil on my desk.

"Yeah baby, almost. I'll meet you at my locker." She looks at me with a disgusted expression before flipping her waist length hair and walking towards the exit. I keep my head low, feeling more insignificant than I've ever felt in my life.

It's something about Tori that makes me hate being me. I wish I was as pretty and popular as she is. I'm sure high school is going awesome for her.

"It's OK, you can go. I'll come up with an idea to present to Mrs. Weaver on Monday."

"No," he speaks quickly, "I want to help. How about we exchange numbers, and we talk about it some more this weekend?"

I look in his dark brown eyes before shaking my head, yes. He takes his phone from his pocket and hands it to me. I stare at the screen saver of him and Tori before putting my number in his cell. I hand it back to him and he presses call, allowing it to ring a few times before his number pops up on my screen.

"Lock me in. I'm serious about this project; I want to help." He stands up and heads to his desk to grab his belongings before walking towards me again. "I have a game tomorrow but I'm free on Sunday. Maybe we can link up then." I stare at him, not knowing what to say. He reads the speechlessness on my face, "I'll just call you."

***

"So... today is the big day!" I smack my lips at Kyra as she mocks me from the other side of the phone. I look in my vanity mirror and stare at my thick coils in need of a serious washing and conditioning.

"Yeah," I mumble, trying not to sound as nervous as I am.

I can't believe I'm supposed to be meeting up with my school nemesis today!

"Has he called yet?" I sigh quietly and glance at my alarm clock sitting on my nightstand. It's after two in the afternoon and I haven't heard a peep from him all weekend.

"No."

"Well, this is Marcus we're talking about. High school athlete and professional butthole. Maybe he's going to stand you up, Les." I sigh again, realizing that she's more than likely right.

He's never been nice to me before, so why should a stupid school project make him start now?

I get off the phone with Kyra and decide to hit the showers. If I am doing this project solo, I need to clean my body and get started right away. I sing along with my favorite song as it blares from my portable speaker. I'm washing my hair a second time when I hear a knock at the bathroom door.

"Yes?!" I yell out, struggling to hear what my mom is saying over all the noise. I hear "mumble, mumble, mumble, school, mumble, mumble" and decide to respond with, "OK!" Honestly, I have no idea what she just said. I'll have to ask her what it was when I'm finished.

I wrap my comfy towel around my body and swing open the bathroom door. I sing the same line of my favorite song repeatedly as I proceed into my bedroom. I jump out of my skin and almost drop my towel when I see Marcus sitting on my bed. He looks almost as embarrassed as I feel.

"Marcus! What the heck are you doing in here?!" I shout. He nervously jumps to his feet.

"Leslie, I'm so, so sorry! Your mom let me in and led me to your room. She said she was going to let you know I was here to work on our school project." I hurry inside of my walk-in closet and close the door.

"Why didn't she have you wait downstairs like a normal parent?" I yell through the door as I pull my underwear up and quickly throw on my sports bra. He hesitates before answering my question.

"I honestly have no idea. It was a couple of ladies sitting on your couch when I walked in. I'm assuming your mom has company." I sigh swiftly after remembering that my mom does have those cackling hens she calls friends over here every other day. I roll my eyes at the thought of their nosy behinds while I pull up my leggings.

"How do you know where I live?" I ask, pulling my T-shirt over my head. I open the closet door before he gets a chance to answer. He stares at me with his mouth gaped open, somewhat making me blush. It almost seems like he is in awe of me but I'm sure I'm hallucinating.

Marcus Tate will never be attracted to me, especially with a girl as beautiful as Tori on his arm.

"Uhh… well, we have known each other for six years. I may have seen you outside a time or two while I was passing by. I honestly can't remember how I know, I just… know."

He chuckles nervously as if his answer embarrassed him. He looks away with an awkward smile. I blush again, even though I'm trying my hardest not to do so. It almost seems like he's been checking for me without me noticing.

Lesley, you're tripping. This is Marcus Tate you're talking about.

I shake the thought away quickly. My hair drips all over my shirt, prompting me to retrieve my towel from my disorganized closet. I flop down on my bed and signal for him to do the same. I pat my moist hair with the towel while Marcus stares at me attentively. I stop after the abnormal spectating makes me feel weird.

"You have a lot of hair. How did I not notice this before?" He uses his fingers to grab one of my coils. He yanks at it gently and then releases it, allowing it to snap back into its naturally curly state. I successfully fight the urge to blush for a third time.

"Because I always wear it in a bun. It's too much hair to do anything else with." He grabs another curly strand.

"It's so soft and thick… I love it. You should wear it like this more often. It's very beautiful." I stare at him until his eyes meet mine. I look away when the gazing makes my heart flutter.

Why is my heart reacting favorably to Marcus Tate???

"Sorry, I don't mean to violate your space. Just couldn't help myself. Did you know my mom is a hairdresser?"

"Wow! No, I didn't know that."

"Yeah, so I know more about hair than I'm willing to admit in public." He laughs and so do I. We lock eyes again, for a little longer this time. My heart nearly beats out of my chest from the intimate-seeming moment.

"Umm, are you thirsty? Hungry?" I break our deep stares to stand to my feet. I head towards my room door as I wait for his reply. I turn around and catch him glaring at me with smitten eyes. He smiles once he realizes that I caught him. My desire to blush finally gets the best of me.

"Uh… yeah, water is good." I nod my head at his request.

"Ok, water it is."

"I turn around and catch him glaring at me with smitten eyes. He smiles once he realizes that I caught him. My desire to blush finally gets the best of me."

Why is my heart reacting favorably to Marcus Tate???

CHAPTER THREE
TOO CRUEL TO BE CLOSE

"So…"

I stare at Kyra while she's trying to be all in my business. I grab my English book before closing my locker.

"So… what?" She smacks her lips at me for playing dumb.

"So! What happened between you and Marcus? Or maybe I should go and ask him." She turns in the direction of Marcus's locker, forcing me to tug her backwards by her shoulders. She turns around and faces me with a huge grin.

"You are such a hot mess! I can't stand you."

"I know, but you love me."

We both giggle before heading towards our English class. My anxiety grows with every step I take towards Marcus's locker. I see him standing at it with Tori and I get a little jealous. I drop my head once we approach the most popular couple in school. Kyra glares at him and then at me. She smacks her lips with shock.

"Did you see what he just did?" I shake my head, no, after we pass them, "Of course you didn't, because as soon as we got near him, you put your head down like you're ashamed of yourself or something. You are too lanky to be slouched over like that. Stand tall, girl! If I stood 5'9, everyone would notice me. Chin up, head in the clouds, confidence on a thousand." She shoots me a warm smile after trying to make me feel better about myself. I eventually give her one back.

Sometimes, I wish I could be as confident as Kyra.

We make it to English class 10 minutes early and settle in our seats. Kyra's desk is positioned directly in front of mine. She spins around in her chair as soon as she sits down. She stares at my hair as if she didn't notice it before.

"Ok! New hairstyle alert! I like it! I've never seen you wear your curls down before."

I hump my shoulders and blush, making it obvious that my dolled-up appearance has something to do with Marcus's visit. She shakes her head, "Tsk, tsk, tsk. It all makes sense now. You're being all secretive about what happened between you and Marcus yesterday, you come to school looking all fabulous today, and when Marcus just saw you in the hallway, he looked at you like you were an ice-cold cup of lemonade on a hot summer's day-"

"Did he, really?" I cut her off to ask. I gawk at her with hopeful eyes. She leans back a little, looking completely surprised by my reaction. She moves closer to me and lowers her voice.

"Ok, we're not going to do this… enough is enough! We're best friends! You don't hold stuff like this from me! I've been waiting forever to hear something this juicy coming from you, so you better spill it!"

I giggle and lean in closer, whispering to her about what happened between Marcus and I yesterday. I tell her about the shower fiasco, him touching my hair, and how much he seemed to love staring at me. Then, I fill her in on how he and I talked for hours about everything but our project, and how we didn't come up with a topic until after he got home and called me because it had gotten so late. We came up with the topic immediately, but we were still on the phone for an hour and a half after that laughing and getting to know each other better.

"…and we still didn't want to get off the phone, but it was almost midnight." I wrap up the story as Marcus walks in the classroom. Our eyes lock instantly, causing my breathing to slow. He makes his way to his seat without breaking our flirtatious glares. Kyra notices our engulfment and looks surprised again. She hits my arm, finally snatching my attention away from Marcus.

"Les, what the heck! What was that?" I hump my shoulders again, providing her with an artificial answer. I smile from ear to ear, "So, what you're trying to tell me is that you like Marcus Tate now? The prick that made most of middle school unbearable for you--- Mr. Jockstrap?"

My smile fades, but I don't reply to her concerns. She takes a deep breath, "Look, I love you, and I want you to be happy, but please, really think about this: All of a sudden, he's being nice to you and getting you emotionally bent out of shape, and for what? For the sake of being nice? Or because he likes you, too? Hecky no! He's using you! You're going to get his embarrassing grade up in science and he's going to go back to being the jerk that he is! I mean, come on! He's in a relationship with the most popular girl in school, Ms. Head Cheerleader, Tori Buchanan. That snob will ruin you if you so much as go near her man. Just be careful with this."

She turns around quickly when our English teacher steps inside the classroom. I let out a long sigh before sliding down in my chair. Even though I don't want to believe her, she is making a lot of sense.

Kyra is right. I'm letting Marcus Tate play me.

***

"Is something wrong?" Marcus inquires, glaring at me from the other side of my living room couch. My eyes are glued to my laptop. I barely acknowledge his presence.

"No. Everything is fine." He hesitates before looking at his laptop as well. I write down a few notes on electrical currents. Marcus looks at me again.

"I really feel like something is bothering you. Is it me?" I glance at him quickly and then back at my notebook. I refuse to answer his question. He sits his laptop on the table and slides closer to me. His leg rests against mine, creating a few electrical currents of our own, "Now I know it's me. You won't even answer my question."

I set my pencil on my notebook before turning to engage with him. I pause once I take in how gorgeous he is.

I can't believe I've never noticed that until now.

He grins like he can read my mind. I get angry for being so transparent. I sit my stuff on the table and stand to my feet. "I'll be right back," I state, walking into the kitchen to get some much-needed space from the stressful environment.

Whatever this is I think is happening between Marcus Tate and me IS NOT REAL! Get it together, Les!

I take a deep breath to calm my nerves. "Seriously Leslie, what did I do?" Marcus's words startle me from behind. I turn to face him, appearing surprised by how close he's standing to me. I immediately take a step backwards.

"Nothing… you didn't do anything. Listen, we don't need to chat about personal stuff to do our assignment. I'm only interested in getting this project done as soon as possible so we can get on with our lives." He stares at me confusedly.

"Get on with our lives? I thought we were working on our friendship?" He takes a step towards me, prompting me to take another step back. My lower back presses against the kitchen counter.

"It's OK, Marcus. You don't have to pretend. We're going to get an '*A*' on this assignment whether you act nice to me or not."

"Act nice? Leslie, what are you talking about?" I break our eye contact while I prepare a proper response.

Should I really go there?

I think I should.

"Our past is very painful for me. You were cruel… extremely cruel. I didn't want to go to school because of you and your friends. You haven't liked me as long as we've known each other so why would you suddenly like me now?" He takes a deep breath before taking another step in my direction. I panic after I realize that I can no longer back away from him. He looks down at me and I reluctantly look up at him.

"What do I have to do to show you how sorry I am about that? It makes me super embarrassed to think about all the things I've put you through over the years. I was an awful person back then, and I'm so ashamed of that."

"But why me, Marcus? You never picked on anyone the way you picked on me. What did I do to make you hate me so much?" He inches even closer to me, which I didn't know was physically possible. I start to breath hard when I feel his chest against mine. He breathes down my neck, causing me to flinch from the feeling. He presses his lips against my earlobe and lowers his talking to a whisper.

"Did you ever think that maybe you had it all wrong? That maybe I picked on you all the time because I *liked* you that much?" He pulls back to look into my eyes. The suspense from the intense moment is killing me. I stumble over sounds, looking for words that I can't find. His sights go from my eyes to my lips.

"BUZZ!... BUZZ!... BUZZ!" The vibration coming from his jean pocket captures both of our attention. He takes out his cell phone, revealing Tori's face on its screen with the words, "My Baby", displayed underneath. I squeeze from between him and the counter when he makes a busted face.

"We should get back to our project after your call," I exclaim dryly. I turn around and head into the living room without saying another word.

"Tsk, tsk, tsk. It all makes sense now. You're being all secretive about what happened between you and Marcus yesterday, you come to school looking all fabulous today, and when Marcus just saw you in the hallway, he looked at you like you were an ice-cold cup of lemonade on a hot summer's day-"

CHAPTER FOUR
WOODINGTON PARK

Tuesday and Wednesday pass without incident and Thursday is wrapping up at this very second. I'd be lying if I said that Marcus Tate hasn't been heavy on my mind all week, but honestly, what difference would it make if he has? I must keep my head on straight if I want to get an *"A"* on this science fair project. Besides, Marcus has someone already, so there is no room for crushes…

Especially if that crush is me.

I pack my belongings in my bookbag just as the bell rings. I'm preparing to leave when Marcus approaches me. "Hey Leslie, I wasn't sure if you got my text or not, but I don't have practice today. I was wondering if I could come over and we could get some more of our project done?" I glance down at my phone and realize that I do have a message from him. I look up and notice Tori walking past us angrily without addressing Marcus at all. Her eyes appear to be stuck on me instead. Marcus's face is uneasy, but he doesn't acknowledge the visible tension between the two.

That's odd.

I tell Marcus he can come over before I find out my mom has company again. I immediately regret my decision as soon as I walk through the front door. I sigh at the sight of the gossiping ladies and attempt to dart upstairs before I'm spotted. My mom calls out my name before I'm able to do so.

Busted.

"Leslie! I know you're not about to be rude and walk in here without speaking! I didn't raise you like that!" I grind my teeth with my back towards her, quickly fixing my face before turning around to acknowledge her and her company.

"Sorry, mom. I didn't mean to be rude. I'm in a hurry to get up to my room and work on my science fair project, that's all. Hello, everyone." I turn around to proceed up the stairs. My foot touches the first step.

"Science fair project? You mean that assignment that you're working on with Brenda's boy, Marcus?" I sigh before turning around to face her and her heavy-set friends again.

"Brenda? You mean Brenda that does hair up the street from the chicken spot?" One of her friends holding a red plastic cup asks. Mom gestures that she is correct.

"Yes mom, that's the project."

"Oh, OK. You seem to be a little sweet on that boy. I don't blame you, either. He is very handsome. If only I were a few years younger." My mom's friends laugh hysterically at her comment. I subtly shake my head at the inappropriate remark. I creep up to my room before she's able to say another word in my direction.

"You mean 50 years younger," I hear one of her friends blurt out, instantly rubbing my mom the wrong way. Mom begins cursing the lady out loudly. I close my room door and flop down on my bed. They have officially ruined my mood.

I can't have Marcus come over here now, especially with those drunk heifers downstairs. I need to cancel.

I use my cell phone to call him. He answers on the first ring.

"Hello?"

"Wow, that was quick," I giggle. "Hey, I'm sorry, I know I said you could come over today, but-"

"No." He cuts me off to say. I make a confused face.

"No? What do you mean, no?"

"I mean, no. I'm not about to let you cancel. I've kind of been looking forward to this since I found out practice was canceled today." I blush so hard that my cheeks hurt.

I'm so glad he can't see me right now.

"I know you're eager to complete the assignment and all, but if you come over here, we won't be able to get much work done. My mom's loud friends are here again."

"That's not what I was talking about, but OK, I understand." I blush again.

I was hoping he wasn't talking about the project.

"Yeah. Sorry."

"What are you sorry for? That just means that you're coming over here. So, when can I expect you?" I giggle at his informal invitation.

"I'm sorry, what?"

"There you go with that word again. How about this: I'll be there to pick you up in 15 minutes. Be ready, please. I'm hanging up."

He disconnects the call, but the phone is still pressed firmly against my ear. For some reason, it's taking me some time to process what's currently happening. I eventually drop the phone to the bed and scream silently with excitement. I head for my closet, deciding to spice up my look with a fresh change of clothes. My goal is to look drop-dead gorgeous without looking like I'm trying too hard.

I really hope I'm able to pull it off.

I ease into a pair of skintight jeans and a flowy, orange blouse. I love wearing orange; it seems to make my tan-colored skin pop. I spray my hair lightly with a water and conditioner mixture to bring some life back to my thirsty curls. I pin one side over with a cute, orange clip and paint my lips with some fruit-scented, glitter lip gloss.

I slide my feet into my brown, heeled, ankle boots and throw on my brown jacket to match. I check myself in the mirror and for the first time in a long while, I'm satisfied with what I see. I grab my notebook and laptop and put them in my oversized, brown purse. I get done just in time for me to receive a text message from Marcus:

He's outside.

I hit my body with my favorite fragrant mist before stepping out of my room. I speed down the stairs and shout bye to my mom. She starts to say something to me, but I'm out of the door before she's able to finish her statement. I figure she'll call or text me if it's important.

I walk towards Marcus's white Mustang, trying my best not to look as excited as I feel. He stares at me blatantly, taking in the sight of me from head to toe. He hops out of his car in time to open the passenger side door.

"Wow," he mumbles when I subtly brush past him. I get inside of his vehicle without saying a word.

"*Mission accomplished,*" I think with a grin. I watch him until he climbs into the driver's seat. He gawks at me for a moment, causing me to blush uncontrollably. He pulls off shortly thereafter. We immediately head towards the freeway.

"Uhh... where are we going? You can't possibly live this far from the school."

"You're right, I don't. I have another destination in

mind. It's a surprise." His unexpected change of plans catches me off guard. He glances at me with dreamy eyes, "Do you trust me?" I look down for a moment, fully taking in the question.

If he would have asked me this a week ago, I would have said hecky no, but now, the only answer I can think of is...

"Yes." He smiles.

"Good. Just sit back and enjoy the ride. We'll be there soon."

***

We pull up to a park lined with dense forest and he eases into a parking spot. I've lived here my whole life and I don't think I've ever been to this place before. He gets out and proceeds to open my door.

"Marcus, where are we?" I ask curiously. I get out of the car while waiting for a reply. He doesn't provide one right away. Instead, he grabs my hand and pulls me towards a small path.

"This is Woodington Park, one of the last barely touched nature preserves we have around here." We follow the trail until we make it to a wooden boardwalk and a beautiful body of water. I notice people fishing but they're few and far between.

"It's a bench right up there," he states. He points in its direction, prompting our bodies to head towards it. Our hands lightly brush against each other's with every step we take. Goosebumps form on every inch of my skin from the electrifying gesture.

We finally make it to the bench and sit down, staring out at the glistening water instead of at each other. After a few moments, my attention goes from the calming sight to Marcus's face. His golden-brown skin seems to glow distractingly underneath the sunlight. I must admit, his manly features are highly captivating. He is so different than I remember him being all those years before.

My number one enemy is turning into my number one love interest.

He finally turns in my direction to acknowledge my passionate glares. He immediately returns the favor, causing an overwhelming feeling to explode throughout my chest. I look away after the feeling becomes too much for me to handle. He places his fingertips on my chin to guide my eyes back to his.

"Why are you so afraid of this?" He inquires seriously. I want to act like I don't know what he means, but he knows that I do.

"I'm afraid that you'll hurt me again," I want to say, but instead, I look away once more. He makes a disappointing noise. The awkward silence tries to draw a wedge between us. He puts his arm around me and pulls me closer to counter it.

"Marcus, what are you trying to do?" I question with bouts of confusion seeping from my voice. He slowly strokes my arm through my jacket, causing more goosebumps to form on my already freckled skin.

"I'm trying to do what comes natural to me, instead of fighting it like I've done ever since I met you." I glance at him, trying to understand what his answer means. He takes a deep breath before giving me his undivided attention.

"I remember the first time I saw you; we were in Mrs. Moncho's class. You remember that?" I smile as the memory comes to mind.

"Yeah, I remember. You walked up to me and told me to get up because I was sitting in your seat, and when I didn't-"

"I pushed you to the floor." He finishes my statement and then takes another deep breath. He looks down before he speaks his next words, "That may have been what really happened, but in my head, something else was going on." He finally looks at me again, "When I first walked in that class and saw your face, my little heart stopped. I had never seen anyone so beautiful in my life, and your smile... your smile was-" I start to blush and he smirks. "There it is. It's amazing."

His face gets serious suddenly, causing me to look at him attentively. "I have no idea why I decided to be so mean to you. It was the first thing I thought to do. Every time you came around me, my palms got sweaty, and my heart started racing. I didn't know how to handle those feelings and that angered me, so I took it out on you instead. It's crazy--- as in love as I was with your smile, I made sure you never wanted to show it to me again."

My heart jumps when I hear the words, *"in love"*, leave his lips. I almost thought he was about to say that he was falling in love with me. I've been waiting forever for a guy to feel that way about me.

It'll probably never happen, though... especially not from a guy as gorgeous as Marcus Tate.

He looks at me as if he wants me to say something, but his confession has me floored. He takes the emotionally heavy moment as an opportunity to move in for a kiss. I panic, deciding to bring up his girlfriend's name before his lips reach mine.

"What about Tori?" He draws his face back, looking bothered by my untimely name drop. He sighs before removing his arm from around me.

"What about her?" He mumbles while looking away. Their relationship is obviously a sore subject for him.

"I was just wondering… I mean, you were just trying to kiss me, but I thought you and her were still together." He fidgets uncomfortably, making me instantly regret my inquiry.

I can literally die from embarrassment right now!

"I didn't mean to ruin the mood," I mutter apologetically. The awkward silence appears again, but this time it engulfs our entire situation effortlessly. I scoot away from him uneasily, "We should probably go now."

I stand up after the unsettling moment gets the best of me. Marcus gawks at me but doesn't follow suit. I sigh and move towards the water, resting my elbows on the wooden rail overseeing the vast body. I stare out at the sparkling waves, enjoying the cool breeze blowing through my hair. The beauty of this place sweeps me away for a second, causing me to render any bad thoughts I may have momentarily had about me, Marcus and our growing dilemma.

The sound of Marcus's footsteps slowly approaching snap me out of my peaceful trance. I glance over my shoulder and spot him coming my way. His 6'3 frame presses against my back once he reaches me. His mouth rests closely to ear. I lean my body against his, feeling his heart beating faster with every breath he takes.

"Your heart… It's about to beat right out of your chest." He takes a deep breath and wraps his arms snuggly around my waist.

"It does that every time you're near. It's trying to get closer to you."

"Hello?"
"Wow, that was quick," I giggle. "Hey, I'm sorry, I know I said you could come over today, but-"
"No." He cuts me off to say. I make a confused face.
"No? What do you mean, no?"
"I mean, no. I'm not about to let you cancel. I've kind of been looking forward to this since I found out practice was canceled today."

CHAPTER FIVE
LATE NIGHT DRIVE

I've been lying in bed for hours, but I can't seem to fall sleep. I toss and turn until I'm unable to take it anymore. I sit up and turn my lamp on. I reach for my artbook located on my nightstand. I smile once my newest masterpiece captures my attention.

Marcus Tate looks just as good on paper as he does in person.

Ever since Marcus took me to the park earlier today, all I've been able to think about is him. The way he looked, the way he smelled, *the way he felt...* I still can't wrap my head around what's going on between him and I.

After our heart-to-heart talk, I feel so much closer to him. I knew I was starting to like him before, but now, I think I'm starting to care more than I'm comfortable with. I don't want to fall for him and he makes a fool out of me... which is highly likely since he's in a relationship already. If this situation goes sideways, I'll never be able to show my face at school again. Like Kyra said, I must be careful with this.

My phone goes off unexpectedly and I pick it up. I smile happily when I see Marcus's name on the screen. I glance at my sketch of him again before reading his text.

"You up?" his message asks. I look at the time and notice it's a little after 10 p.m.

"Yeah. How did you know?" He texts back immediately.

"Because I see your light on." I stare at the message with startled eyes.

Is he sitting outside of my house or something?!

"Calm down, I'm not a stalker. I was out for a late-night drive, and I noticed that your light was on. I couldn't sleep." I read his follow-up message and giggle to myself. This does seem a little stalkerish of him, but I still find it kind of sweet.

"Why couldn't you sleep?" I text back, climbing out of bed to look out of my window. I see his white mustang parked across the street and grin cheekily.

"Honestly, I can't get you out of my head. That beautiful smile of yours made my day." I blush so hard that my face hurts. His next message chimes in, "I want to climb up to your window, but I'm sure you won't let me." My stomach turns with nervousness.

He wants to sneak into my room in the middle of the night?!

I hesitate before responding, "You know you're too tall to be climbing through my window. Someone will see you." I nibble on my lip after sending the message. I hear a car door close while waiting for a reply. I look out of the window again and see Marcus darting across the street. He cautiously proceeds to the side of my house. My heartbeat reacts to the thrilling situation.

What does Marcus Tate think he's doing?!

Another text message comes through before I'm able to figure it out. "Come to your back door."

I don't think twice. I hurry out of my room but slow down once I reach my squeaky, wooden stairs. Terrified of waking my mom, I move down them as quietly as possible. I rush towards the kitchen and spot a silhouette of Marcus through the backdoor window. My heart reacts to the shadowy hint of him.

I swallow hard as I approach the door. I open it carefully, trying my best to minimize the squeakiness of the door's hinges. His perfect smile pierces through the darkness of night. I nearly melt from his presence.

"Hi," he says shyly. He awkwardly stuffs his hands in his pockets as if this late-night secret meet-up wasn't his idea. I open the screen door to let him in.

"Hey," I whisper softly, looking into his eyes. We stare into each other's souls for some time, connecting on a level that I never knew existed. He steps closer to me and wraps his arms around my waist.

"I've been thinking about holding you like this again since I dropped you off earlier. I want to kiss you so bad." I bashfully look away when I remember that I've never kissed anyone before. He notices my apprehension and comments on it, "I'm sorry if that makes you uncomfortable. It's just that after our encounter earlier, I told myself that I would always tell you what's on my mind, no matter how crass it may sound. If I would have done that before instead of bullying you, then I might've been with you and not *her*."

He says "her" in a dismissive way, causing me to raise an eyebrow. I'm not sure what's been going on between him and Tori, but I decide I finally care enough to pry.

"Marcus, you never answered my question before. What's up with you and Tori? You guys were like, class couple goals." He shakes his head disappointedly before releasing me. He rubs the back of his faded haircut after leaning against the sink.

"We broke up."

I make a shocked face, immediately wondering what could have happened between them that would have forced them to break-up after all this time. He glances at me before he continues, "I guess it's been over for a while now. We just weren't strong enough to let it go."

"But why? You guys have been together since we were sophomores." He sighs loudly and looks towards the kitchen window.

"You know, it's crazy how things can change so quickly. Back then, all I cared about was football; making the varsity team… becoming captain… going undefeated all season, but once all that crap happened, I discovered that it didn't make me as happy as I thought it would." He stares up at the moon, allowing his thoughts to sweep him away for a second. I move closer to him.

"Why do you think that is?" He looks at me the way the leading fellow looks at his conquest in the movies. I blush nervously at the thought of being his leading lady. He stares at me intensely.

"Because, all of that doesn't matter if I don't have someone by my side that genuinely cares about me to share it with." I look confused by his statement, prompting him to go into depth, "When Tori and I first started dating, we had a lot in common. She wanted to make the cheerleading team, and I wanted to make varsity. We fed off each other's energy, which made us inseparable, but once we started to reach our goals, she started acting different… stuck up even… and I hate people like that."

He sighs quickly before continuing, "I was able to overlook it for a while, but once she made head cheerleader, things took a nosedive. Her cockiness made her so unrecognizable sometimes. Plus, she started caring about her status and her team more than she cared about me. I mean, I get it. I love my teammates, too, but they will never be more important than my relationship." I nod my head at him as if I understand, even though I've never had a team or a relationship before. He grabs my hand and squeezes it tightly. He gazes deeply into my eyes. My knees get weak by his actions.

"What I need is a woman that's smart, beautiful, funny, and down to Earth." His attention goes from my hand to my waist. He softly pulls me into him. I take in the smell of his masculine deodorant after he tightens his hold on me, "What I need is a woman like you."

My mouth falls open once his last words leave his lips. He passionately slides his fingers through my tight curls. He leads my lips towards his. I close my eyes excitedly as I anticipate my first kiss.

I can't believe this is really about to happen!

"Leslie! You down there?" My mother yells from the top of the stairs. I panic, pushing Marcus away before his lips can successfully touch mine.

"Uhh, yeah mom! I just needed a drink of water!" I shove Marcus towards the door and open it quickly. He steps out of the screen door.

"Well… I guess we'll have to finish this some other time," he whispers with a smirk. I smack my lips, giving him the thumbs up after his sly remark. I close the door before he's able to say anything else.

Marcus Tate looks just as good on paper as he does in person.

CHAPTER SIX
EXTRA BAGGAGE

My head is gone, and I know it is. Kyra is talking, but I can't hear a word she's saying. We move down the hallway as a duo even though I'm by myself on cloud nine. Everything is moving in slow motion. Everywhere I turn, I see Marcus's face.

Is this what infatuation feels like, or is this something else?

"Yeah, and also, I decided to cut all of my hair off and dye my scalp blue."

"Mmhmm girl, that's dope," I mumble, clearly ignoring everything that Kyra is saying. She stops moving to grab my arm. Her sudden actions snap me out of my love spell.

"OK, but for real… you're scaring me now."

"What are you talking about?" I try to ask with a straight face. I turn away from her immediately afterward.

I've never been a good liar.

She sees right through me and smacks her lips. Her arms fold in an irritated way, "I'm really trying not to take all of this deceit personally, but you're giving me no choice here." I sigh loudly before looking at her. I'm in too good of a mood for one of her lectures. I'm on a natural high right now and I don't want to be brought down.

I've never felt this way before and dang it... I want to enjoy it!

"I'm sorry if it seems like I'm being deceitful because I'm not trying to be. I'm just... you know..."

I can't find the words, so Kyra rolls her eyes. We eventually start moving again, continuing to the lunchroom in forced silence. We make it inside of the cafeteria and head straight for the lunch line. She faces me while we wait.

"Look... I get it, I really do. Let's not forget, I was with Blake... and then, John. Oh yeah, and we can't forget about Thomas, with his fine self; but yeah, I've been exactly where you are now. I'm so glad that you get to experience those butterflies in your stomach, but I guess my point is that they don't last." She moves with the line before continuing, "And those guys I was with had no extra baggage, but with Marcus, there's a huge sack of luggage--- and it has pom poms."

I shake my head at her as we get within arm reach of the food. I stare at the pizza and the meatball surprise and decide on the pizza. She grabs a plate of pizza as well, "Les, I'm not trying to tell you what to do, but I don't want to see you crying over this, either. You know how you feel about public humiliation; if this blows up in your face, you'll never want to come back to school again." Kyra verbalizes my thoughts from last night and I feel awful. I can't get mad at her for saying exactly what I'm subconsciously feeling. I mean, she does know me that well.

Maybe I am setting myself up for failure.

We grab salads and a soda before heading to our regular table. Right after we sit down, I pull out my hand sanitizer. Kyra sticks out her hand, signaling for me to squeeze some in her palm.

"I'm really upset with Marcus now," Kyra states randomly. She rubs the sanitizer all over her hands.

"More upset with him than usual?" I joke. She narrows her eyes at me.

"Yes, more than usual! I can't believe he's leading you on like this even though the whole world knows he has a girlfriend."

"Actually, when he came over last night, he told me that they broke up." Kyra makes a shocked face and I smirk.

I'm happy to finally burst her bubble for once.

She stares at me for a second before something behind me catches her eye. She shakes her head and grabs her pizza. "Are you sure about that?"

I turn around and immediately see what she's talking about. Marcus and Tori walk into the lunchroom holding hands! My heart sinks into the deepest part of my stomach.

I can't believe Marcus Tate lied to me last night!

He spots me gawking at them and looks away immediately. I turn around to face Kyra, who is glaring at me amusingly. "Now, what were you saying about him not having a girlfriend again?" she asks facetiously. My throat burns at the thought of eating my words. My eyes want to tear up, but I successfully fight the urge.

"Excuse me, I'll be back," I mumble in a low tone. I stand up and rush from the lunchroom. I walk towards the girl's bathroom with rage-filled steps. I need to make it to a stall before my emotions get the best of me.

"Leslie! Leslie, wait!" I hear Marcus's voice coming from behind me. I act as if I don't hear him. He jogs in my direction until he's able to stop my stride.

"Wait, please… give me a chance to explain." I try to walk around him repeatedly, but he gets in my way every time.

"No need," I spit out nastily, refusing to make eye contact with him. I must have been a fool to believe that he and Tori actually broke up.

I'm not going to cry… I'm not going to cry… I'm not going to cry…

"Please, Leslie. I want to." I take a deep breath before finally engaging with him. He grabs my hand and leads me down an empty hallway. He leans against a locker without letting go of my hand. He gently rubs it once he starts talking, "I know how that looked, but I want you to know that it's not what it seems. She and I are not back together, I promise. She thought it would be a good idea to act like a couple until the Spring Formal was over. We've had our outfits for a while, so we decided that it's best for us to still go together."

I snatch my hand away from him after I hear his stupid explanation. He grabs me by my waist this time, "Leslie, I swear to you, I'm not lying, and after the dance is over, her and I are done on all levels. I promise you… as soon as that happens, I'm coming for you. Nothing will be able to stop me." I take a step away from him, letting him know that I refuse to be second on anyone's list. He looks at me as if he doesn't understand where my attitude is coming from.

"What's the matter? I'm standing here being completely honest with you and you're acting like I'm lying or something." I shake my head and fold my arms.

He really doesn't get it.

"Have you even tried to look at this from my point of view?" He stands there for a second, preparing to speak before he thinks. I place my hand up to cut him off, "No… seriously Marcus, have you tried?"

He pauses and rests his back on the locker. He stares at me when his wheels start to turn. We stand there in silence until he quietly maneuvers through his thoughts. He sighs before closing his eyes and laying his head against the locker.

I think he's starting to get it now.

"You must think I'm trying to play you," Marcus states in a low tone.

"Are you?" I have to ask.

"No! I would never try to play you, Leslie. Actually, I-"

"Les, there you are! I went to the bathroom and everything to look for you! Are you OK?" I look down the hall and see Kyra walking towards us. Marcus opens his eyes to glance in Kyra's direction and she gives him an evil glare. He turns away from her quickly.

"Yeah, I'm good. I'll be back in the lunchroom in a second." She stops and puts her hand on her wide hips.

"But I know you're starved, and lunch will be over in five minutes," she exclaims sternly. I sigh at her attempt to separate Marcus and me. Her stares are so intimidating that I decide to head back to lunch with her.

"Marcus, it's OK. Do what you want. I'll see you after school." I take a few steps towards Kyra before pausing to acknowledge him once more, "And I think it's best for us to start meeting at the library instead of my house from now on. I don't want people to get the wrong idea about us."

I turn around and immediately see what she's talking about. Marcus and Tori walk into the lunchroom holding hands! My heart sinks into the deepest part of my stomach.

I can't believe Marcus Tate lied to me last night!

CHAPTER SEVEN
THE FIRST KISS

Marcus stares at me instead of researching his part of our project. I try to concentrate on my reading, but his gawking is distracting the heck out of me.

"Marcus, come on. This project is due in 10 days and we're barely done with the introduction," I say quietly, trying not to interrupt the other people in the library.

"I'm sorry, but how do you expect me to concentrate when I'm sitting across the table from someone as beautiful as you?"

I smack my lips at his compliment to stop myself from smiling. He flashes his pearly whites, causing me to blush against my best efforts. I start to giggle until I spot Kyra eyeballing me. She's sitting with Brandon a few tables away from me and Marcus. I straighten up once I remember what she and I discussed after lunch. She said she would be here for me to "offer moral support", but coming from Kyra, that really means "cock block whenever necessary".

"Look Les, I'm sorry for not considering your feelings with this whole 'me and Tori' thing. I know this situation is messy, but I still meant every word I've ever said about me and you." My heart skips a beat when he calls me Les.

He has never used my nickname before.

"I think it would be best if we didn't refer to 'us' anymore until after the Spring Formal," I blurt out, trying my best to stick to what Kyra and I agreed was the best thing for me to do. Marcus sighs with disappointment before finally looking down at his book. I look down at my book, too, wishing there was an easier way to deal with all of this.

"So, speaking of the Formal, who are you going with?" I sigh at his inability to do his work and I get embarrassed by his question. The truth is, I don't have a date for the Formal.

No one ever asked me.

"I'm not going." He makes a surprised face.

"Why not?" I sigh again.

"Because, I don't have a date." He glances down at his book again, looking regretful for bringing up the topic.

"I would have gone with you if you weren't taking your ex-girlfriend."

We sit there awkwardly, pretending to read over our course materials. After reading over the same paragraph repeatedly, I realize that every intention I have of concentrating has officially gone out of the window. I stand up from the table, which quickly grabs Marcus's attention.

"You aren't leaving yet, are you?"

"No. I just need to find another book."

I lie swiftly before turning around to walk away from him. I disappear down an aisle, taking a deep breath once the coast is clear. Even though I'm pretending to stare at the sea of books before me, I'm not processing any of their titles. My solo stroll is an attempt to put a little space between me and Marcus Tate.

His captivating demeanor is easily penetrating every defense I thought I had against him. I need a chance to regroup and remind myself why it's in my best interest to stay away from him. My valedictorian status is on the line, and I've worked too doggone hard to let some guy I hated three weeks ago jeopardize that with his complicated drama.

"You just wanted to get away from me, didn't you?" Marcus's voice echoes from behind me. I turn around and face him after he startles me.

He seems to be good at that.

My guilty eyes answer his question before my mouth can. I still try to deceive him anyway. "No. I just… I needed a different book." Marcus glances at the novels around us and makes a weird face.

"For our project? Because we're working on electrical currents and you're in the aisle about teen pregnancy." I look around quickly and realize he's right. I instantly grow red with embarrassment. I try to turn away from him, but he stops me before I can, "Les, just talk to me. We're working on our friendship, remember? You don't have to keep things from me, especially when what's bothering you is about us." I take a deep breath and close my eyes tightly.

I want to open up to Marcus, but how can I ever trust him?

"I don't know what to say-"
"How about what you're feeling," he cuts me off quickly to suggest. I look as if a cat has my tongue.

Should I put myself out there, or should I save face?

He notices my inner turmoil and continues, "Listen, I care about you… a lot, and I really care about what you think and how you feel, especially if it has something to do with me. So please, talk to me." He walks up to me and grabs me around my waist like he usually does. I've never had a guy touch me this much, but I can't think about that right now. I take a deep breath and decide to go against my better judgement.

"I don't know. I guess I thought we had something special, but when I saw you with Tori, I figured that I imagined it all. We couldn't possibly be as close as I thought we were if you were holding hands with her."

I look away from him with every word I speak, feeling extremely uncomfortable during this very vulnerable moment. He grabs my chin and directs my eyes towards his.

"We do have something special, and if you had to question that, then I'm messing up big time. Tell me what you want me to do, and I swear I'll do it." His words burn a hole in my soul with the passion behind him. I melt like butter in his hands.

"Do whatever your heart tells you to do," I suggest shyly. I want to stick with me and Kyra's plan, but the truth is, I'm too comfortable in Marcus Tate's arms to put up much of a fight. He immediately stares down at my lips while licking his. I should be nervous, but I've been daydreaming about him kissing me ever since he tried to do so at the park. He moves in and I close my eyes. I wait for his lips to press against mine…

And then…

They finally do.

He kisses me so gently that my knees get weak. He holds me tighter, prompting me to wrap my arms snuggly around his neck. He slides his tongue between my lips, and I gasp shockingly.

I can't believe I'm French-kissing Marcus Tate--- and it feels amazing!

"Leslie!"

The sound of Kyra's voice makes me pull away from Marcus immediately. I glare behind Marcus and see her and Brandon standing there with similar expressions on their faces.

"Girl, we need to talk NOW!" She shouts, causing the library patrons to shush her. She walks towards me quickly and grabs me by the arm.

"Bro… really? What about Tori?" I hear Brandon ask Marcus as Kyra drags me out of the library. I let her lead me inside of the girl's bathroom before snatching my arm from her tight grip.

"Dang, Kyra. That hurt."

"It needed to hurt! I can't believe you, Les! I mean, what the heck were you thinking?!" she asks hysterically. I look taken aback before getting defensive.

"First of all, you need to calm down. I don't understand why you're so up in arms about this, anyway. This has nothing to do with you."

"Calm down? You're telling me that I need to calm down when you're the one acting like a slut and chasing behind someone else's man!" My mouth falls open in disbelief.

I can't believe my best friend just called me a slut!

I fold my arms offendedly as my anger goes from zero to 100. "Slut? I know you're not calling me a slut when you let every guy that looks your way stick his hand down your pants!" Kyra gasps loudly and pauses as if her feelings are hurt. I somewhat feel bad for going there but she started it, not me.

"You're just jealous because I get more male attention than you! That's why you had to make yourself available to the first neanderthal that smiled at you… with your tall, awkward behind!"

I gawk at her, clearly furious about the insults she's throwing my way. She ignores my stares as she continues, "That's why he's using you! He doesn't want you! Him and Tori are going to laugh at your desperate behind once all of this is over and you're not going to have anyone to cry to, not even to me! I mean, who only has one friend? That's pathetic!"

The palm of my hand violently finds the side of Kyra's face before I realize what's happening. She holds her stinging cheek with a shocked expression on her face. I look shocked, too, but I don't say anything. Instead, I storm out of the bathroom after smacking the heck out of my best friend.

"We do have something special, and if you had to question that, then I'm messing up big time. Tell me what you want me to do, and I swear I'll do it."

CHAPTER EIGHT
THE FIRST DATE

I jog in a disheartened manner towards the library to gather my things. I want to fall apart so badly right now, but I'm having the hardest time processing everything that just happened.

I finally had my first kiss, and it was from my number one arch nemesis, Marcus Tate! And to top it off, my best friend and I just got into our first real fight!

I hurry from the library and rush out of the school. I waste no time moving swiftly towards my house. Tears blow from my cheeks with every gust the wind makes. My emotions are at an all-time high and I have no idea how to deal with them.

I can't wait to make it home and climb underneath my covers. I'm experiencing the type of mental emergency that only my bed can fix.

I walk in a distraught fashion with serious tunnel vision. I'm so determined to get home that I never see Marcus pulling up next to me. "Hey. Get in, I'll give you a ride." I hesitate at the sound of his voice, but I never stop moving. I clean my face with the back of my hands.

"No thanks. I'm alright," I spit out dryly. Marcus smacks his lips at my response.

"Leslie… please. I really need to talk to you."

"Later, Marcus. Now is not a good time."

"So, you're just gonna kiss me, make me fall in love with you, and then diss me?" I stop in my tracks after I'm unable to believe what I just heard. My jaw nearly drags the ground. He stops his car as well.

"Wha- What did you just say?" I'm barely able to ask. He grins at the question.

"Baby… get in."

My heart bursts with an explosion of disbelief when he calls me baby. I'm so shocked by his words that my legs refuse to move. After noticing my mannequin-like state, he hops out of his car.

"You heard me. I'm falling in love with you, and I thought you should know… but if you don't want to get in the car with me, then I won't make you." He gives me a hypnotizing glare as he invades my personal space. He caresses my cheek with his hand before kissing me a second time. He pulls back and stares at me again as if he's waiting for a reply.

"I love you, too."

Wait… what?!

He smiles from ear to ear, "Well then… get in the car, woman! I can't have my girl out here walking. Plus, I want you to go somewhere with me." I gawk at him with a surprised expression, barely absorbing anything he's saying right now.

I'm his girl, too?!

He leads me to the passenger door and opens it for me. I slide in, still trying to figure out if I'm in a parallel universe or not.

That would explain all the crazy stuff that has been happening today, that's for sure.

As soon as he gets in the car, he pulls off. I stare out of the window, feeling giddy, overwhelmed, and perplexed all at the same time. He eventually places his hand on mine. I nervously turn in his direction.

"What's on that pretty little mind of yours?" He inquires, glancing at me while he drives.

"Honestly, too much to put into words," I admit. He looks at me again.

"Please baby… try. I'll listen to you talk forever." I blush as I process his sweet statement. I take a deep breath once I decide to trust him with my personal information. I begin to fill him in on the issue I'm having with Kyra. I tell him about her stance regarding him and I being together. I even describe the moments that led up to her getting slapped. He shakes his head after I finish talking.

"Dang, Les. I'm sorry that you and your best friend fell out because of me." I sigh before staring out of the window again.

"I don't know. I thought she would be happy for me because I finally have someone special in my life. Instead, she constantly brings up you and Tori."

"Tell me about it! I'm having the same problem with Brandon, except Brandon is friends with Tori just like he's friends with me. He told me he was going to tell her about me and you, and I said, 'So what!' Tori and I aren't together anymore. Who I'm dating now is none of her business." His words make me feel uneasy.

If Tori finds out about me and Marcus, she's going to come for my head for sure!

"Baby, everything is going to be OK," Marcus assures me with a squeeze of my hand. "I want to be with you and only you, and nothing is going to get in the way of that."

***

Marcus walks me to my door, holding me so tightly that I can barely walk straight. He finally lets me go once we reach the porch.

"Sorry about that. I had no idea you were allergic to seafood." I giggle.

"It's OK. At least you got me out of there before I swelled up like a pufferfish." He smiles and shakes his head.

"But you did like the Mexican food, right?"

"Of course. It's my favorite." We blush at each other like the smitten teenagers we are.

"I'm not ready for this night to be over, but I have a game tomorrow, and coach is really strict about us getting a good night's rest before game days." I nod my head and check my phone, realizing that it's almost 10p.m., "And speaking of tomorrow's game, I was hoping you would come to watch me play." I make an uncomfortable face.

"I don't know, Marcus. I don't like being around my classmates unless I have to be. Plus, Tori will be there-"

"Baby, forget about her. I know I have." I smack my lips at his statement.

I know he doesn't think I believe he's over their relationship already.

"So… what about the Spring Formal, then? I thought you were going with her?" He smirks before pulling me into him.

"Why would I go with her when you're my girlfriend?"

I'm so flattered by his declaration that it shows all over my face. He leans in to kiss me without warning and I let him. Our lips dance slowly while my hands rub the back of his fade. We make-out like love-sick youngsters until my front door swings open.

"Good night, Marcus," my mother exclaims sternly before turning the porch light on. She startles us both, forcing us to let go of each other immediately.

"Umm, good- goodnight, ma'am," he stutters before taking a few steps away from me. She folds her arms and narrows her eyes at him.

"Good night," I say to him embarrassingly. I rush into the house and close the door.

I can't believe my mom just humiliated me like that!

"Leslie, what was that all about? You're out all times of the night and being intimate with boys now?" My embarrassment turns into anger, but I try my best to control it.

"Mom, what do you mean all times of the night? My curfew is at 11p.m." She glances at the clock on the wall and realizes it's only 10p.m.

"Oh… well, I forgot. I'm not used to you being out past dark." I roll my eyes in my head before turning around to head upstairs.

"What about that kiss? That was a very passionate smooch. Do I need to be worried about you being alone with that boy?" I stop in my tracks, unable to control my anger any longer. I spin around quickly to face her.

"Worry about me being alone with him? Mom, I'm about to be 18 years old!" My mother looks taken aback by my tone but doesn't comment on it. I take a deep breath and check myself because I hate being disrespectful.

"Mom, I didn't mean to get loud, but I'm not a child anymore. I know you're not used to me having a personal life, but I have a boyfriend now." I smirk to myself after my last statement.

I still can't believe that Marcus Tate is my boyfriend!

"I know you're getting older, and I know I have to respect that, but before he can officially be your boyfriend, I need to have a talk with him first." I nod my head at her request.

"No problem, mom. That can be arranged."

I finally had my first kiss, and it was from my number one arch nemesis, Marcus Tate! And to top it off, my best friend and I just got into our first real fight!

CHAPTER NINE
THE SCIENCE FAIR SWITCH

I linger in the back of the stands, looking like a fresh fish out of water. On top of me having no idea what I'm looking at, I also had no idea that every person here would be wearing the same colors.

I'm sticking out just like a sore thumb, which is exactly what I was afraid of.

What I have been noticing, however, is the way the crowd reacts to everything Marcus does. Every time he throws the ball to someone, everyone goes crazy. I want to cheer for him as well, but I'm far too uncomfortable to do so. I keep my distance from the rest of the school by sitting in the very last row. I smile as I watch him have his moment. I can't believe my boyfriend is the quarterback of an undefeated team.

I love him.

I watch the game confusedly and pay close attention when the crowd cheers. I make mental notes of the plays that get the most positive feedback. I secretly try to learn about football for the sake of my new relationship. We're winning by 21 points. I think Marcus's undefeated title is safe.

"We're going to the championship with a perfect record!" The commentator shouts, causing the crowd to go wild. I jump up from my seat when everyone else does. The spectators chat happily as I slide past pupil after pupil. I decide to head towards the field to congratulate my boyfriend on a great game.

"Excuse me! Excuse- pardon me!" I exclaim until I reach the bottom of the bleachers. I see a sea of uniformed players and at first, I can't tell which athlete is Marcus. I move closer to the team until I spot Tori and the cheerleaders mingling with the guys. I stop in my tracks and fold my arms once Marcus comes into view.

She's over there with my man!

I keep my distance but watch their interaction closely. Their conversation appears to be a negative one. They seem to be having some sort of argument. She tries to grab his arm, but he snatches away from her. She gets upset and storms off. I let out a huge sigh of relief before proceeding towards him. He finally sees my face and waves.

"There's my girl," Marcus says with a smile. I blush as I make it over to him.

"Hey! Great game. Can't act like I know what was going on exactly, but I see that we won." He laughs at my ignorance.

"Yeah... we won, and we're going to the 'ship!" He exclaims happily. I smile as he takes me in his arms and pecks me quickly. His teammates rush over and grab him.

"Baby, I'll call you later!" He screams while the players drag him away. I smile like a proud girlfriend and wave bye to him. I watch him until he disappears from my sight. I turn around to head for the exit. I'm approaching the gate when Tori and a few of her cheerleading sidekicks step in my path.

"So... you're Marcus's new girlfriend, huh?" She spits out distastefully. I make an alarmed face.

I'm so not ready for this confrontation yet!

"Uhh…" I mutter, not knowing what to say. My head goes down like it usually does whenever Tori is around. I'm so nervous right now, I could vomit. The cheerleaders look at each other and laugh.

"Ladies, she can't be. He would never choose someone like her over me. She's too ugly and insignificant to be with someone like Marcus." They laugh even louder when they bump past me. I'm trying my hardest not to cry, but I can't fight it. I hurry towards the exit before anyone notices my tears.

"Hey! Leslie, wait up!" I wipe my eyes with my sleeves. I turn around quickly and see Brandon behind me, but I decide to keep walking. "Leslie, hold up a second. I just want to talk to you." I reluctantly slow my roll so that he can catch up with me. I rub my face again to wipe away any evidence of my sorrow. I notice he's still wearing his black and red Cardinal's football uniform when he approaches me.

"I just wanted to talk to you really quickly and see if you had a date to the Spring Formal." I look at him weirdly.

"What do you mean? I'm going with Marcus." Brandon shakes his head.

"Really? Because he just told me that he's going with Tori." I look confused.

"No. He's going with me. He said so last night."

"Well, I talked to him just now, and he said that Tori was begging him and making him feel all bad and whatnot, so he decided to take her instead." I take a deep breath, trying not to let Brandon's rumor upset me more than I already am.

"Well, I don't believe you." I turn around and walk away before he's able to say another word. I can't deal with this drama right now. I take out my phone and call Marcus as I hurry towards my house… no answer.

What have I gotten myself into?

***

I call and text Marcus all night, but he never answers or responds. I wake up in the morning and check my phone, feeling dumber than I felt last night.

He has gone all night without returning any of my calls or texts. Maybe Kyra was right… he and Tori were probably together after the game poking fun at me for being so gullible.

My phone goes off and I grab it quickly. It's a text message from Marcus. *"Finally,"* I think, before opening it to read it.

"My bad about last night. Things got crazy with the team. I meant to call you, but it got really late. I need to tell you something about the Spring Formal. I'm sorry baby, but I can't go. A family thing came up. I promise, I'll make it up to you. I have practice in a few minutes. Coach is riding us hard about the upcoming game. I'll link up with you when I can to finish the project, but I don't know how much free time I'll have with the championship happening in less than a week. I'm sorry about dumping all of this on you via text, but I promise I'll call you later. Love you."

I read over the message twice before attempting to reply. I type four different messages but can't bring myself to send any of them. I go from believing him, to calling him a liar, to accusing him of still being in a relationship with Tori, to saying he's full of crap entirely. I honestly don't know what to think.

This would be the perfect time to get advice from a friend. If only I had one…

I lay in bed longer than I usually do, trying to make sense of my Marcus, Brandon, Tori, and Kyra dilemmas.

Why did Brandon ask me about the Spring Formal last night? Was it just to rub it in my face that Marcus is taking Tori instead of me?

But Marcus just said he wasn't going, so who's telling the truth?

I sigh out loud and decide it's time to do something productive. That's the only way I'm going to get all this drama off my mind. I need to work on this science fair project. That should keep me occupied.

***

I stand in front of my locker, feeling like I could pass out at any second from the amount of anxiety I'm feeling. I have situations with so many people going on at once that my head is spinning. Marcus never called me yesterday and I have yet to see him at school today. I'm starting to think he's avoiding me.

Why else would I have not heard from him by now?

I saw Kyra for a split second, but she turned around and went the other way once she saw my face. I'm not looking for Brandon or Tori. One run-in with them and I'm liable to go home early.

The bell rings, and my stomach starts to turn. I must make it through an entire school day battling with my emotions about people that I'm forced to look at in every class. I take one look in my first hour and notice Kyra sitting in her regular seat in front of mine. I quickly decide that I can't do it. I head straight for the principal's office instead. I need to convince him that I'm sick and I need to go home. I'm not a good liar, but technically, I'm not lying.

I can throw up at any second.

"Ms. Thompson, how can I help you?" I look at the secretary uneasily.

"Umm... I was wondering if I could talk to Principal Tate?" She glances behind her and notices his door open.

"Just one second." She gets up and sticks her head in his office, says a few words to him, and walks back to her desk.

"Yup, he said he has time. Go right in." I walk around her desk and head into his office. He looks at me and smiles.

"Well, if it isn't my best and brightest." I smile back awkwardly and sit down after he signals for me to do so. "I'm not used to seeing you in here, so this is a pleasant surprise. How can I help you?"

"Uhh…" I swallow hard. I had a whole script in my head before I got here, but now I can't remember a single line of it. "It's about my science fair project… I'm having a hard time with it."

That wasn't what I rehearsed! How can I complain to him about his own son?

"Oh? What seems to be the problem? Is your partner giving you a hard time?" I swallow hard again but decide to just come right out and say it.

"Yes. I'm not receiving much help. I ended up doing most of the project by myself yesterday." Principal Tate makes a confused face.

"That's weird. You and Kyra have always worked so well together. Why are you ladies suddenly having issues now?" My eyes grow to the size of saucers.

Did he just say that Kyra is supposed to be my partner?!

"I'm sorry Principal Tate, did you just say that you think Kyra is my partner?"

"Yes. Hasn't she always been?"

"Yes! But Mrs. Weaver said that you picked the partners this year because some students needed passing grades to graduate." Principal Tate looks confused.

"What? That makes absolutely no sense. If students are failing, that's their own fault. They need to make up their grades on their own time. I would never intervene with the science fair projects, and I would especially never break you and Kyra up. Your partnership represents this school every year at the convention!"

I sit there in awe, not understanding what's happening. He stares at my facial expression before he continues, "Well, who are you working with, then?" I look at him and take a deep breath before answering.

"Marcus."

"Marcus? My son, Marcus?" Principal Tate gets angry and stands up quickly. "Marcus works with Brandon every year." He puts on his suit jacket, "Well, who the heck is working with Brandon?"

"Kyra." He shakes his head and grabs the bridge of his nose.

"Come with me. We're about to straighten this whole thing out right now."

He has gone all night without returning any of my calls or texts. Maybe Kyra was right... he and Tori were probably together after the game poking fun at me for being so gullible.

CHAPTER TEN
THE LESLIE RACE

Principal Tate talks to Mrs. Weaver a few feet from me and I immediately tune them out. I stare at Kyra standing on the other side of the hallway against the lockers, but she doesn't look in my direction.

"Ok ladies, sorry about that." Principal Tate starts talking to us both and Kyra and I move towards him. "It seems that Brandon and Marcus conjured up this whole plan. They are the ones that gave Mrs. Weaver that made-up science fair partners list. I don't know what their intentions were, but I'm going to get to the bottom of it."

His deep voice is filled with anger, but he still manages to give us a half smile. "How about you ladies go to the library and work on your project now? I'll let your teachers know that you have a special assignment to complete. I don't care if it takes you the rest of the week to get it done, you will be excused from every class every day. You girls make this school very proud every year at the convention. I know the same thing will happen this year." He smiles at us again before walking towards Mrs. Weaver, towering over her with his giant stature. Kyra and I stand there awkwardly until I finally decide to break our silence.

"Look… Kyra… I'm sorry. I was completely out of line for putting my hands on you the way I did." Kyra looks at the ground and humps her shoulders.

"Maybe I deserved it. I should have been more of a friend and less of a dictator." She finally looks up at me.

"No. You were right, evidently. Marcus played me, just like you said he would. Just another one of his cruel jokes." We turn and slowly head for the library as I fight back tears. Kyra notices and rubs my arm.

"Les, I'm sorry. I know how much you liked him." I stop walking in the empty hallway as the faucets in my eyes turn on. Kyra grabs me and hugs me, "Come on, don't do that, stop. It's OK."

"No, it's not!" I whine sadly. "He told me he loved me, and I believed him! How stupid can I be?!" The bell rings and Kyra quickly leads me to the bathroom before the other students flood the hallway. I stand in front of the mirror as she goes inside of a stall to grab me some tissue.

"Well, well, well… if it isn't Ms. Man Stealer herself." I gawk at the door and see Tori standing there. I turn away to clear my distraught face. The sight of me weeping seems to throw her off.

"Why are you crying? Shouldn't that be my job?" She looks in the mirror and wipes something from her flawless face. I look at her weirdly.

"What do you mean, 'your job'?"

"Marcus left me for you. I should be the one that's balling my eyes out." She looks bothered before looking down quickly, trying to control her emotions.

"What? No. It was all a stupid joke. He doesn't like me for real." She looks at me through the mirror with glossy eyes.

"As much as I would love to agree with you, I can't." She sighs before pulling her lip gloss from her purse, "Marcus has had a thing for you for a long time, even before him and I got together. I knew about it, but I tried to ignore it." She pauses to apply it over her already shiny lips, "But eventually, I couldn't take it anymore. The way I used to catch him looking at you sometimes," she halts and glances over at me, "He never looked at me like that." I stand there confused, not knowing what to say. She sighs and turns to face me. "Look, I know I've been a world-class witch to you, but that was just me being jealous. Marcus wanted you; he never wanted me. I was just too proud to let him go. Sadly, I probably would have ridden out our empty relationship if he wouldn't have broken up with me first."

She humps her shoulders, "I guess what I'm trying to say is that I'm sorry for being so mean to you. That probably wasn't the best way to go about things, but now that it's over between him and I, I can finally move on. We all can." She smiles at me awkwardly before hurrying out of the bathroom. Kyra opens the stall door, making the exact same face I'm making.

"Wow," she mutters, staring at me through the mirror. "At first, I thought she was going to come in here with her girls and start tripping! I was ready to run out of the stall and start clocking bimbos! But then... wow." She comes back to her original statement, and I shake my head in agreement.

Tori Buchanan... jealous of me? I never would have guessed it!

Kyra and I walk into the library, deciding to go to a part that's rarely used by anyone. We know that we can get privacy over here. We have so many things that we need to catch up on.

We talked for the first two hours about everything but our assignment. She tells me about how torturous it has been to work with Brandon, and I tell her about how things went with Marcus. We vent nonstop until we notice Brandon heading our way. He walks over to our table and makes an uncomfortable face.

"Hello, ladies." We stare at him, refusing to speak back. Kyra folds her arms and Brandon takes a deep breath, "Look, Principal Tate told me that I needed to come apologize, so I wanted to tell you ladies that I'm sorry. I didn't mean to cause this much confusion, but for the record, the switch wasn't my idea, it was Marcus's." Kyra rolls her eyes at his words.

"Whatever, Brandon-"

"No wait… I want to hear this," I cut Kyra off to state. She looks bothered at first, but then secretly checks herself.

This is a friendship, not a dictatorship.

Brandon looks at us both before sitting down at the table with us. "I'm just going to be honest: A few of us on the team… well… we sort of have a crush on you, Leslie." He looks at me with serious eyes and I blush unexpectedly. I feel surprisedly flattered as he continues, "Your name has come up a lot in practice, especially lately. We've almost made it through our entire high school career and not one of us has ever dated you. We've dated all the other pretty girls in school, some of us have even shared girls--- no offense, Kyra." She rolls her eyes at him, "But anyway, you were the one that no one could get with, which put you high on the list of most desirable dates for the Spring Formal." I look at him like he's crazy.

"The one that no one could get with? None of you ever asked me out." He chuckles and shakes his head.

"Asked you out? Do you think that we have to ask these girls out?" I smack my lips at his slimeball comment. He backtracks, "I didn't mean it like that. What I'm saying is that most of the pretty girls care about status more than anything else. We're the best football team this school has ever had; we're undefeated, for heaven's sake. We were mentioned in the newspaper, on the radio… we've even been on tv a couple of times. Chicks seem to dig that crap." I fold my arms displeasingly, "If you're into that type of thing, that is." He realizes he's talking himself into a corner and stops.

"I believe you had a point," Kyra spits out impatiently.

"Oh, yeah." He clears his throat and looks at me, "A few of the fellas mentioned one day that they were going to ask you to the dance, but Marcus didn't like that. We all knew that he's had the biggest crush on you since, like, middle school or something, but he was also dating that fine honey, Tori, so he was automatically disqualified from the Leslie race. He waited until practice was over to pull me to the side and asked me if I wanted to work with Kyra this year for the science fair project. I told him heck yeah at the time because I knew that I would get a good grade and my GPA needed it. He told me he would set everything up, so I didn't think twice about it. It wasn't until I overheard him arguing with Tori after the game the other night that I realized what was really going on. He told her that he didn't want to be with her anymore because he was with you now, and that's when my dumb self finally realized that he only wanted to switch so that he could get closer to you."

He chuckles and shakes his head, "That slick son-of-a-gun. That's when I asked you about the Spring Formal and you pretty much confirmed everything that I thought. By the time I got into the locker room, the news of him sneaking and snatching you up made it around to the other players. They were not happy with him going behind their backs the way he did; especially since he was already tagging the most popular chick in school. Just greedy."

He shakes his head again, "I actually thought it was brilliant, though… and pretty darn funny." He chuckles again, but Kyra and I don't see the humor in his recollection of events. We stare at him until he stops.

"So, if you knew what you knew, why did you tell me that he was taking Tori instead of me?" He smiles at me and rubs his fingers through his curly hair.

"I still wanted my shot. You can't blame a guy for trying." He humps his shoulders and Kyra and I look at him disgustedly.

"Ugh! You're such a jerk, goodbye!" Kyra shouts, causing him to stand up with a smirk. He walks away from the table without saying another word.

We talked for the first two hours about everything but our assignment. She tells me about how torturous it has been to work with Brandon, and I tell her about how things went with Marcus.

CHAPTER ELEVEN
ONE WITH NATURE

Kyra and I sit there for a while, discussing all the craziness that's happening. We are so shocked by our drama that we can't stop talking about it for another few hours. We finally get it out of our system enough to discuss our science fair projects, recapping what we were working on with Brandon and Marcus.

"Excuse me ladies, I don't mean to interrupt, but did Brandon come in here to apologize?" Kyra and I stare up at Principal Tate and nod our heads yes, "Ok, good." He tries to walk away, but he hesitates. He turns around and addresses us again. "I was wondering, have you heard from Marcus today? He never showed up for school, and the coach hasn't seen him, either. I called his cell and the house, but he's not answering. I'm really worried about him. It's not like him to do this type of thing, especially during championship week." I pull out my phone and look at it, but I don't have any missed calls or texts from Marcus. I dial his number and place the phone up to my ear, but he doesn't pick up.

"Sorry Principal Tate, but he's not answering for me, either." He sighs before looking disappointed.

"OK, but if you happen to hear from him, please tell him to call me." I grin and gesture that I will. He finally turns and walks away.

"Dang. I wonder what that's about. I hope he's OK," Kyra says, sounding like she's really concerned.

"Do you, really?" I ask as my text alert goes off. I look down at my phone and notice a message from Marcus.

"I'm sorry, baby. I have a lot on my mind. I needed to be one with nature today." I read over his message as Kyra responds to my question.

"Of course I do!" I smile at her.

"I'm so glad you said that girl, because I need a ride somewhere."

***

Kyra and I pull up at Woodington Park and I immediately spot Marcus's car. We hop out and I lead her towards the path.

"Wow… look at this place. It's gorgeous," Kyra admits, looking up at the majestic trees. "How do you know about this place, Les?" I grin and look over at her.

"Marcus brought me here." Kyra smiles at me warmly before taking in the forest some more. I think she's finally allowing herself to be happy for me.

Thank God.

We follow the same trail that Marcus and I took the last time we were here. The huge body of water comes into view first, and then I see Marcus sitting on the bench where he and I were sitting before. I stop walking and grab Kyra's arm.

"Hey, there's Marcus." I point in his direction. She turns her head to follow my finger. "I need to talk to him alone. I hope you don't mind." She grins and nods her head as if she understands.

"No problem. I think I see a cute guy standing over there by himself, anyway," she responds. I giggle before shaking my head at her. We go our separate ways shortly thereafter. I walk slowly towards Marcus, sighing heavily to myself. I want to be mad at him for creating all this drama, but honestly, I just miss the heck out of him.

Is this really what love does to people?

I make it to the bench and stand over him. "Is this seat taken?" I ask, prompting him to look up at me. He appears shocked to see me at first, but then slides over to make room for me. He stares at me while I sit down.

"How did you get here?" he questions, sitting up to get more comfortable in his seat. I glare out at the sparkling sight before answering.

"Kyra brought me."

"Oh, where is she?" I look down the boardwalk and spot her standing next to some guy in the middle of fishing. I point in their direction. "Oh, OK. I see she's able to make new friends anywhere." We both chuckle lightly before our old friend, awkwardness, makes an appearance.

"Marcus…" I say, pausing to find the words I'm so desperately searching for. There are so many questions that I want to ask, but I don't know where to begin.

"Les, I think I owe you an apology." He takes a deep breath before staring out at the water, "I did something stupid, and I feel terrible about it. Now, everyone is mad at me for it."

"Are you talking about you creating the fake list that swapped our science fair partners?" He looks at me with a shocked expression.

"You know about that?"

"Yeah. That… amongst other things." He sighs as he breaks our eye contact.

"Baby, I'm so sorry about that. I don't know what I was thinking."

"I have a pretty good idea of what you were thinking, thanks to Brandon." He leans forward to place his face in his hands. He takes a deep breath before staring out at the water again.

"Dang-it! Not Brandon… Man, I can only imagine how that story went with his ignorant way of thinking."

"Well, it was… interesting." He shakes his head, "But I would really love to hear it from you." He glances at me.

"Ever since that damn flyer about the Spring Formal went up, that's all everyone has been talking about, especially my teammates. You'd be surprised at the stuff they say when we are in the locker room having unfiltered conversations." I shake my head.

"I'm sure it sounds a lot like Brandon." Marcus disagrees immediately.

"Oh no. What you heard was definitely the PG version of what Brandon would have said if you were one of the guys on the team. Believe me… you have no idea." I make a disgusted face, "But anyway, all they cared about was who they were taking to the dance, and since the team has literally ran through every other pretty girl in the school, they had their eyes set on you. I couldn't let that happen."

"Why couldn't you?" He turns his body towards me.

"You want the truth?" I nod my head yes, "Ok, well, to be completely honest with you, they were trying to see who could sleep with you first. That's all they care about. It's a game to them. They have a bet going to see who can have sex with the most girls on the 'acceptable list' before school is out. You are the only girl left on the list." I look at him with an offended expression.

"Ugh! I can't believe y'all! That's despicable."

"No, don't say 'y'all'. I've had the same girlfriend since I started varsity. Heck no. My mother raised me better than that." I stare at him weirdly, prompting him to think about his words, "Well, I *did* have the same girlfriend. I have a new one now."

He smiles at me, but I don't smile back. He makes an uneasy face, "You are still my girl, right?" He puts his arm around me and stares into my eyes, but I don't answer him. He kisses me sweetly and my skin tingles.

"Yes, I guess I'm still yours." He smiles again.

"I'm glad." He kisses me a second time before continuing with his story, "When I noticed them making serious plans to pursue you, I had to step in. It's no secret that I've always had a thing for you, but that wasn't the reason why I came up with the fake science fair partners list. My main goal was to protect you from them, but that was going to be hard because, well, you hated my guts."

"Big time." I chime in, and we laugh.

"We had to be friends before you would trust anything I said, so that's where the list idea came from. I figured that if we were forced to work together, then I could make you like me. I'm very charming when I want to be." He smiles and I giggle, "But I should've known that us getting closer would make me want to act on all the old, harbored feelings I had for you. I swear, I wasn't trying to coerce you into being with me. It just… happened." He sighs and I sigh as well.

I can't believe he went through all of this just to protect me from his teammates.

"So, what happened at the game? I haven't really heard from you since then." He takes a deep breath before straightening up in his seat and staring out at the water again.

"Everything hit the fan. Brandon told Tori that he caught you and I kissing in the library, and she flipped out. I ignored every attempt she made to contact me but immediately after the game was over, she walked up and confronted me. She wanted to fight about it, but I dismissed her. I didn't have to explain anything to her; she wasn't my girl anymore, you were. I think she was just mad because she wasn't the first one to pull the plug on our dying relationship."

"Her and I had a moment in the bathroom today," I add, throwing my two cents in our convo. He gawks at me.

"A moment? What did she do?"

"She actually apologized to me for being so mean." Marcus makes a shocked face and I giggle, "She said that she always knew that you had a thing for me, but she didn't want to believe it. She said she's ready to move on." He looks pleasantly surprised by Tori's actions.

"Well… that was decent of her. I still don't trust her, though." I giggle again.

"Yeah… I talked to Brandon that night after the game, too. He was trying to ask me if I would be his date to the Spring Formal." Marcus rolls his eyes at the news.

"That vulture." He shakes his head, "I wouldn't be surprised if he asks Tori to the Formal. I think that's the only reason why he hung around us so tough. He was waiting for me to turn my back so that he could swoop in and snatch her up."

"Does that bother you?" He takes a deep breath before looking at me seriously.

"It does, but that doesn't mean what you think it means. I just hate it when people pretend to be your friend, but they have a hidden agenda-"

"You mean, just like you did to me when you switched our science fair partners?" I cut him off and he narrows his eyes at me. I laugh at my joke, and he finally laughs, too.

"Exactly! Just like what I did to you." We laugh even more at his facetiousness. He sighs before going back to his story, "Evidently, a few of my teammates overheard Tori and I arguing, and they told the rest of the team that I was dating you. They were not happy about me messing up their little plan. It was a long, after game locker room argument about me and you. The whole thing was crazy. It was me vs.

the entire team. I've never been so angry in my life. That's the reason why I couldn't call you. My head was all jacked up." I listen to him attentively.

"So, is that why you skipped school today?"

"Yeah, and no." Sadness comes over him before he continues, "When I texted you about me not going to the Formal, I had just found out that my mom needs to get surgery on her spine. It's scheduled for the exact same day as the dance. They said she won't be able to walk for a while, so my dad and I will have to take care of her." I rub his back as my heart aches for him and his family. "So, mix that news with everything else that's been going on, and I just couldn't do it today. I mentally couldn't handle anything stressful happening at school. I know I would've snapped." I look at him lovingly.

"Is there anything I can do?" He looks at me the same way.

"You can tell Kyra that you're leaving with me. I really need you right now."

"Wow... look at this place. It's gorgeous," Kyra admits, looking up at the majestic trees. "How do you know about this place, Les?" I grin and look over at her.
    "Marcus brought me here." Kyra smiles at me warmly before taking in the forest some more. I think she's finally allowing herself to be happy for me.

Thank God.

CHAPTER TWELVE
S.E.X.

Between coming up with a whole new trophy-worthy project with Kyra and being an attentive girlfriend to Marcus, I'm more tired than I've ever been in my life. He told Mrs. Weaver that he couldn't work with Brandon, so I agreed to still be his partner, too. Thankfully, I did most of the project on Sunday, so Marcus should be able to handle the rest by himself.

"No, Kyra. That's tacky. Why not put it here instead?" Kyra looks at me and rolls her eyes.

"Les, I'm trying to be patient with you, but you are really starting to get on my nerves!" I place my hands on my hips.

"I just want it to be award-winning. What's wrong with that?"

"Nothing is wrong with it… except for the fact that I'm already science-faired out. After I leave you every day, I meet up with Brandon to do the exact same thing, and unlike Marcus, Brandon is extremely stupid." I shake my head and laugh at Kyra, but she doesn't think it's funny.

"I'm sorry, girl. I get it, and I feel your pain. I couldn't imagine having to see this thing through with Brandon. I still don't understand why you didn't say no when he asked you to still be his partner." She sighs and picks up a piece of border for the board.

"Honestly, it was the money. He offered me $300 to keep working with him, and let's be honest, I could use some new clothes." We both laugh.

"OK, this is going to have to do." She secures the last piece of the border before we both take a step back and look over our work. I'm not ecstatic with it but I'm kind of tired of all this science fair madness myself.

"This is officially the last day we have to work on it. The championship game is tomorrow and the Spring Formal is Sunday, and then our projects are due on Monday." Kyra shakes her head as if she knows already.

"Speaking of the championship game, has Marcus decided if he's going to play or not?" Kyra inquires while sitting down at the library table. I sigh before sitting down as well.

"He hasn't talked much about it. He hasn't even been to practice at all this week. I don't think the backup quarterback is any good, though, so he may still play."

"Backup quarterback? Look at you learning football terms!" I smile cheekily.

"And he may not have been practicing football, but I'm sure he's been practicing something else. There isn't a waking moment when you two aren't together outside of school. Plus, with the way y'all stare at each other in class, I know something nasty is going on." I smack my lips at her accusations.

"Kyra, stop it! You know doggone well I'm still a virgin."

"Yeah, but for how long?" I shake my head at her, "You are dating the captain of the football team. You know how popular he is, and ever since the news of him and Tori breaking up went viral, I can't look in his direction without some skank throwing herself at him. I know you see it, too." I sigh and roll my eyes because I know exactly what she's talking about. Even though everyone knows that I'm his new girlfriend, they still can't keep their hands off him. It's evident that Tori demanded way more respect than I do.

"I definitely notice, but I also notice him dismissing the heck out of them as well. Most of the time, he won't even respond to their advances. He tells me every single time it happens, too. As much as I don't want to hear about it, I respect his honesty and his desire to tell me everything. He says I'm his best friend. I trust him." Kyra smiles respectfully at my words.

"That's really dope, Les. I'm so happy that you're happy." I smile back at her.

"So, what's up with you and the Formal? Did you decide on a date?"

"Girl, yes!" She gets giddy, "And you will never guess with who."

"Who?"

"Girl, Thomas!" I make an unpleasant face.

"Even after everything Brandon and Marcus told us about that filthy football team, you're still going to go with Thomas?"

"Hey, don't pass judgment. You are dating the captain."

She has a point.

"And I know things didn't work out with me and Thomas last time but he is just so freakin' fine!" She shivers and I giggle.

"Well girl, do your thang!"

"So, will I see you and Marcus there?"

"No. That's the day of his mom's surgery. I probably won't even see Marcus that day myself." Kyra nods her head with understanding.

"Alright then, girl. Let's take this project to Mrs. Weaver's room. We've been in this part of the library so much that they should name this section after us." I laugh at her words as she folds up the board and I grab everything else. We leave the library and walk towards our science class.

***

"I'm so glad this science fair crap is over with," Marcus says, taking a sip from his water. I take a fry from his plate and he smacks his lips at me. "Really? If you wanted fries, why didn't you just order some?" I smile at him.

"So, what you're saying is that I can't have any of your fries?" He smiles back at me.

Of course you can, baby. I'll share anything with you." I blush before addressing his original statement.

"Yeah, I can agree with you about the science fair. I mean, it used to be so fun, but this year it was nothing short of a headache." Marcus makes a guilty face.

"I'm sure that had a lot to do with me." I grin.

"Yup, you might be right." He takes a deep breath and stares at his food. I notice his mood taking a negative turn, so I take another fry from his plate. He looks at me and chuckles.

"You know, I said share, not you can eat them all. You owe me some lovin' for every fry you hijack." I smile, but his words remind me of what Kyra said earlier and it fades quickly.

"Marcus, does it bother you that we haven't talked about… you know?" He bites his burger before looking at me curiously. He stares at me until he finishes chewing.

"You mean, sex?" I nod my head yes shyly.

"No, it doesn't bother me. Why? Does it bother you?" I pick up a crouton from my salad and toss it in my mouth.

"Well, it's not that it bothers me, but it's no secret how popular you are, and it's always a crowd of girls around you, and I'm sure they've been propositioning you-"

"Let me stop you right there. Did you hear what you just said? It's always girls around me, and yes, they do offer things to me, but do you see how easy that is to stumble across? Sex can be the bomb, but it's overrated as heck. Especially when you can get it from almost anyone nowadays. You're just so different from everyone else, Les, and that's what I love about you. We have gotten to know each other without sex even being in the topic cards. There are an infinite number of things to talk about without sex being one of them. I'm a guy. I enjoy working for it, but these new aged girls, let's just say they're nothing like my momma." He takes another bite of his sandwich and I grin at his words.

"Speaking of your mom, how is she?" Marcus looks at me before standing up and sliding his plate across the table. He sits next to me and puts his arm around me.

"I just now realized that I'm sitting too far away from you. I haven't touched your perfect skin in almost 20 minutes." I look at him and smile before he gives me a quick peck. I rub his leg before grabbing my fork. He always does this when he doesn't want to talk about something. I decided to respect his conversation block.

We get quiet to allow each other the time to eat. After we finish, he signals for our waitress and requests the bill. She gathers our plates and trash from the table. She walks away as I decide to bring up another topic that I'm curious about.

"So, what are you doing tomorrow?" I try to indirectly ask him about the championship game, and he smiles at my poor attempt to beat around the bush.

"Waking up, calling you, eating, picking you up, and taking you to the game with me."

"Taking me to the game? I didn't know we were going." He looks at me seriously.

"I didn't work this hard all year to not play in the championship game. I'm taking that trophy home. And plus, my backup is trash. We won't score a point if he plays." I drink the rest of my soda before we get up from the table. He leads me to the restaurant's exit and holds the door open for me to walk out first. We get in the car, but he doesn't start it up. He stares at his steering wheel with a troubled expression.

"Les, I need you." I look over at him and grab his hand.

"I'm here." He looks at me with vulnerable eyes.

"I know I ask a lot from you emotionally, but the next couple of days are going to be extremely hard for me." He looks away suddenly as he tries to fight back tears. I rub his back lovingly.

"Marcus, I'm serious. I'm here in any way that you need me to be." He grabs my hand and kisses it as his tears begin to run down his cheeks.

"I'm just scared. I'm scared that I'm not going to see this thing through. I'm afraid that I made it this far with a perfect record just to lose it all in the end. My teammates and I aren't on the best of terms so I'm afraid that our lack of chemistry will kill our chances of winning tomorrow." I rub the back of his head as he continues, "And my mom." He puts his hand up to his face and cries harder. I reach over and wrap my arms around him, trying my best to console him. He buries his face into my arm, "I'm terrified for her. She's never had to go through anything like this before. They know she won't be able to walk right after the surgery but there's a chance that she will never walk again. What if she's stuck in a wheelchair for the rest of her life?"

"Babe, you can't think like that. You have to be hopeful and trust that everything will be OK." I hold him tighter as he cries freely, releasing all his pinned-up emotions on my shoulder. He finally pulls himself together enough to let me go. He starts his car after wiping his face with his shirt.

"Wow, I must really love you. I've never cried like that in front of anyone but my momma." He sniffs and chuckles. I giggle as well.

"I'm glad, because I love you, too."

"And he may not have been practicing football, but I'm sure he's been practicing something else. There isn't a waking moment when you two aren't together outside of school. Plus, with the way y'all stare at each other in class, I know something nasty is going on."

CHAPTER THIRTEEN
THE CHAMPIONSHIP GAME

I sit on the front bleacher right behind the Cardinal's bench, which is where Marcus begged me to sit. I hate being this close to everyone, but Marcus said he needs to be able to look up regularly and see my face. He claims I give him that extra boost of confidence that he needs.

The game is going well. We keep scoring first, but the opposing team always scores right after us. The game is really close. This place is packed and the fans on both sides of the field are having the time of their lives. Even the mascots and cheerleaders haven't sat down yet. I am so out of my element being here.

"Halftime! The score is tied at 14! This is going to be a good one, people!" The commentator talks loudly over the speakers while the teams head towards their respective locker rooms. Marcus locks eyes with me and smiles before disappearing down the tunnel. The fans in the stands start getting up and moving towards the bathrooms and the concession stands. I stay put and pull my phone from my purse.

"Hey girl! I knew you were here!" I look up and see Kyra walking towards me. I smile at her.

"Hey! What are you doing here?" She grins and sits down.

"Trying to support Thomas-"

"I know, with his fine self." I finish her statement and we both laugh.

"I see that Marcus decided to play. That's how I knew you were here. Y'all are conjoined at the hip."

"Ha-ha-ha," I spew out sarcastically, causing her to giggle. "So, where are you sitting?" She turns around and points towards a couple of girls.

"With Brit and Angela. They're here to cheer on their Spring Formal dates as well." I wave at them, and they wave back. "Well, OK girl, let me get back to my seat before all those people start coming back and someone steals it. I can't believe the crowd out here tonight!" I shake my head as if I can't believe it, either.

"I know! It is the championship game though, and like Brandon said, they are the best football team this school has ever had." She rolls her eyes at the sound of his name while standing to her feet.

"Alright Les, I'll see you later." She heads towards her friends and I stare at the teams returning to the field. They walk over to their respective benches and Marcus heads straight for me. He looks angry and I begin to worry. I stare at him as he approaches.

"Hey, you OK?" He throws his helmet to the ground before sitting next to me.

"Man, coach and the team are on some bullcrap! The backup just threw a fit because he's been practicing all week but isn't playing. He said it's not fair that I didn't show up for practice at all but I still get to start, so the coach is benching me for the second half."

"What! He can't do that!"

"Well, he is, especially since the team agreed. They would rather lose the game than let me play. I swear man, they're a bunch of idiots!" I put my hand on his.

"Babe, it's OK. They're going to put you back in the game, especially if the backup is as bad as you say he is." Marcus looks at me and shakes his head.

"Man, but still! Me? Benched? This mess is unbelievable!" His coach signals for him to rejoin the team. He picks up his helmet and jogs in their direction. I watch their interaction and Marcus throws his helmet down again. He flops down hard on the bench and puts his face in his hands.

The third quarter is embarrassingly awful. The backup quarterback throws one interception and fumbles twice. The score is now 28 to 14. We are officially getting our behinds kicked. The crowd starts to yell at the coach about Marcus's absence from the game. He ignores their shouting and booing until Principal Tate walks up to him. They have a heated conversation on the sidelines and then Marcus's dad walks away. The coach calls a timeout and puts Marcus back in the game.

"Woohoo!" I start to cheer along with everyone else once we see Marcus run out on the field. He looks angry before smashing his helmet on his head. There are only two minutes left in the third quarter, but somehow Marcus still manages to throw a touchdown. The crowd goes wild again as we close our losing gap down to a touchdown.

The fourth quarter starts and Marcus goes to work. He gets another touchdown out the gate and officially ties the game. The other team kicks it into high gear as well and they drive it to the endzone. Now, they're up by a touchdown again.

"Come on, babe, you can do this!" I yell at Marcus. He gets back on the field and moves the ball with our team's running back. We eventually make it to the endzone and Marcus runs it in for another touchdown. I stand to my feet and cheer loudly for my man.

The teams go back and forth with the scoring again, with the score reading 42-all. The commentator talks excitedly over the intercom.

"It's crazy! We've officially broken the scoring record! No team has ever gotten 42 points in a championship game! We've just made school history tonight! Let's give it up for our amazing team!" The crowd goes wild while we all stand to our feet.

Marcus leads the offense on the field with a minute and 20 left on the clock. Marcus moves the ball, throwing for short yards and he finds his man every time. We near the endzone with 27 seconds left and Marcus finds his man yet again. Brandon catches the ball and runs for the endzone. A player from the defense catches Brandon and strips the ball from his hand, before turning around and running with it in the opposite direction. The guy moves fast, weaving through the players on our team. Marcus turns around and chases him down the field.

"He's at the 50! 40! 30! 25..." the commentator gives us second by second coverage as Marcus catches up with him. He tackles him to the ground with three seconds left on the clock.

"Timeout!" The opposing coach yells and the clock stops. He calls for his defense to leave the field as he sends out the field goal unit. Marcus jogs off the field looking like he's ready to choke the life out of Brandon. My heart sinks as I realize that we could lose the game. The players from both teams line up on the field as the kicker sends the ball in the air.

"And it's good! The Lions win the championship!" The opposite stand roars loudly and runs from the bleachers onto the field. Marcus jumps up quickly and heads for the tunnel. His teammates follow behind him in defeat. Everyone standing behind me is disappointingly quiet. We can't believe we just lost the championship game on our own field.

I stand by the gate as the teammates start to emerge from the locker room. I hear a bunch of people saying good game as they walk towards the exit holding their duffel bags. I see Marcus coming and I take a deep breath. I know that the ride home is going to be a rough one. He spots my face and smiles. He looks surprisedly happy as he approaches me and kisses me sweetly.

"Baby, you are so beautiful." I look at him with a surprised expression.

"Thanks, babe. I must say, you're a little more chipper than I thought you'd be." He wraps his arm around me and we walk towards the parking lot.

"I know we lost, but it wasn't my fault. I actually played one of the best games I've ever played tonight, so I'm proud of myself." I look at him and smile.

"I'm proud of you, too." He smiles back.

"Plus, you should have seen everyone's' faces when we got to the locker room! They all agreed to sit me down and that's what ultimately led to us getting our butts kicked. I had a huge 'told you so' moment once we stepped off the field. It felt so freakin' good, too." We make it to his car and he throws his football stuff in the trunk. He stares at me for a second until he closes it. He walks over to me with a silver bag in his hand. I look at it curiously.

"This is for you. I hope it fits." I glance at it, noticing orange fabric protruding from it. He holds the bag for me while I pull out the stunning dress equipped with spaghetti straps and rhinestones.

"Oh my gosh! Marcus, this is gorgeous! But what is it for?" I put the dress back in the bag and he grabs me around the waist.

"I know tomorrow is a big deal for my family, but it's also our Spring Formal. I'm going to be at the hospital all day, but I was hoping that maybe you'd go to the Formal with me after my mom's surgery is over." My face lights up and so does his. "I'm really going to need to be around you after everything that's happening tomorrow, so I might as well show you off while I do it. You're the most gorgeous girl on the planet." He kisses me and I delightfully accept. We happily jump in his car before he pulls off.

I sit on the front bleacher right behind the Cardinal's bench, which is where Marcus begged me to sit. I hate being this close to everyone, but Marcus said he needs to be able to look up regularly and see my face. He claims I give him that extra boost of confidence that he needs.

I'm his good luck charm.

CHAPTER FOURTEEN
THE SPRING FORMAL

I walk down the stairs bashfully as I see my mom, her friends, and Marcus staring at me.

"Oh my God! She looks so beautiful!" One of her friends state, causing me to blush. My mom starts fixing my dress the moment I reach the bottom of the steps.

"Thanks everyone, but you really didn't have to go through all this trouble. It's the Formal, not the prom." Everyone laughs.

"Leslie, please. They were probably going to be here, anyway," my mom mentions. Her friends nod their heads in agreement. I giggle.

I look over at Marcus standing near the door wearing a cream suit with orange trim. We stare at each other with identical expressions as we take in how perfectly the other person looks. He finally walks over to me.

"Baby… you look…"

"Ditto," I respond, agreeing with whatever it is he's about to say. My mother and her friends smile.

"OK y'all, have a great time!" I grab Marcus's hand as we head towards the door, "And don't forget, I still want to talk to you about dating my daughter, young man!" I shake my head at my mom before walking out the door.

I knew she was going to say that.

We get into the car. I glance at Marcus again, admiring how handsome he looks in a suit. He feels me looking at him and glances at me as well.

"You look absolutely stunning in that dress. I'm so glad I bought the right size. I was so nervous about it being wrong." I look down at the gorgeous garment.

"This is a beautiful, beautiful dress, Marcus. What made you get orange?" He smiles at the question.

"I remembered the first time I picked you up when we went to the park, you had on that orange shirt. I thought you looked so gorgeous in that color; it complimented your skin perfectly, just like it's doing now." I blush as he states my exact feelings on the color. He starts his car as I respond.

"It's crazy that you say that, because orange is my favorite color."

"It should be. It's lovely, just like you." I blush harder once I realize that I have the sweetest boyfriend on this side of the universe.

We continue to hold hands while he drives towards the school. We walk inside after he finds a close parking spot. The school is packed from the moment we step inside. I start to feel uneasy again, not liking being around this many of my classmates for the second night in a row. Marcus takes me by the hand and leads me towards the gym. We walk in and immediately bump into Brandon and Tori. It's obvious that the two are on a date. Everyone appears shocked by what they're seeing.

"What's up, Marcus… didn't expect to see you here," Brandon spits out cockily. Tori snatches her hand away from Brandon and looks away embarrassingly. Marcus stares at Brandon with an angry expression on his face. The tense moment is too much. I decide to intervene.

"Babe, let's go and find a seat. I don't want my feet to start hurting before I get a chance to dance," I make up quickly. I drag Marcus away from Brandon and Tori and head towards the table where Kyra and Thomas are sitting.

They are so engulfed in each other that they don't notice us approaching them.

"Hey, y'all."

"Oh my gosh! Hey, Les! I thought you said you weren't coming!" Kyra stands up and hugs me tightly.

"Well, you know… things change," I reply with a grin. Marcus sits at the table with Thomas, but they don't say anything to each other.

It seems like the entire team has beef now.

Kyra and I notice their tension immediately but we try our best to ignore it. "Are these seats available, or…?" I ask hopefully. Kyra makes a disappointed face.

"Sorry, girl. Brit and Angela are sitting there. I wish I would've known you were coming; I would have definitely saved you a seat." I nod my head at her in an understanding way.

"It's OK, girl. It's no big deal." I tap Marcus on his shoulder and he stands up. "Sorry babe, but these seats are taken."

"I'm cool with that," he exclaims, trying to hide his growing irritation. He takes me by the hand and leads me to the punch bowl. He pours a cup and hands it to me before pouring his own. I put the cup up to my lips and sip the red concoction. I make a weird face as the sour flavor offends my taste buds. Marcus glances around the room but doesn't sip his punch. He appears extremely uncomfortable. I rub his back to calm his nerves.

"Babe, you know we can leave whenever you're ready." He fakes a smile.

"I'm good. It's our Formal. I want us to have a good time." I look at him seriously.

"We don't have to be here to have a good time. You know how much I hate public gatherings and you have a lot on your mind right now. I just don't think this is the best environment to be in-"

"Oops! My bad, bro," Brandon says after he aggressively bumps into Marcus. Marcus's punch spills all over his cream suit. I turn around hurriedly to grab a pile of napkins.

"Oh my God! Marcus, stop!" I hear Tori yelling, causing me to divert my attention to what she's referencing. I gasp once I see Marcus on top of Brandon. He punches him repeatedly, prompting me to run over and grab his arm.

"Marcus! That's enough! Get off him!" I shout. Marcus stops swinging as soon as he hears my voice. He darts through the crowd and heads straight for the exit. I follow behind him as closely as I can. He slows down once he nears his vehicle.

He angrily paces back and forth instead of getting inside of his car. I stare at him worriedly, not knowing what I should say to make him feel better. I watch him until he calms down enough to speak.

"I'm sorry that I lost it, but he's been asking for it," he growls out. I listen to him without saying anything. I don't agree with using violence to solve an issue, but I did slap my best friend not too long ago, so I have no room to judge.

"Marcus! You butthole! You broke my nose!" We both look towards the school's entrance and see Tori helping Brandon out of the door. Brandon holds his head back with a huge wad of bloody tissue underneath his nose.

"You better be glad it wasn't your jaw," Marcus roars before toughly moving towards Brandon. I jump in front of him to impede his feisty plan. I grab his face to get his attention.

"Marcus, let's just leave."

"Yeah, Marcus. Do what your girlfriend says and get out of here before-"

"Before what?" Marcus spits out, trying to move me out of his path to charge towards Brandon again. I stop him once more.

"Brandon… let's just go, please!" Tori finally chimes in as she tugs him towards their ride.

"Naw… it's about time to get everything out in the open don't you think, bro?" Marcus grinds his teeth at the question.

"I have no idea what you're talking about!"

"Oh, you don't? That's interesting. Maybe these text messages will jog your memory." Marcus's eyes get big when Brandon retrieves his phone from his pocket. I make a confused face.

What the heck is Brandon talking about?

"Come on, bro. Let's not do this here," Marcus pleads in a softer tone. I look around and notice a crowd growing around us.

"Bro? Oh, so I'm your bro again, huh? Naw… It's too late for that now." Brandon pulls up his text history:

"Me: 'What's up, bro? Have you finished the list yet?'

Marcus: 'Yeah, we can take it to Mrs. Weaver tomorrow. This switch is going to be hilarious. They have no idea what's in store for them.'

Brandon chuckles and shakes his head, "Hold on, let me scroll down to our text messages after the game last week." Marcus reacts unfavorably to Brandon's actions. He tries to get to Brandon again and I'm unable to stop him this time. He moves me out of his way easily.

"Marcus, stop! I want to hear this!" I shout at his back. Marcus stops before he gets to Brandon and drops his head in defeat. Kyra emerges from the school just as Brandon starts reading his message history again.

"Me: 'Dang, bro! The team was on your head last night! They weren't feeling the way you snatched up Leslie like that.'

Marcus: 'Yeah, I know. I needed to prove a point. I didn't even want her like that and I still pulled her. I thought it would be hard because I used to torture the heck out of her back in the day, but it was surprisingly easy. She's a lot more gullible than I thought.'

Me: 'So you hit that yet?'

Marcus: 'I'll smash her after the Formal, and then y'all can have her.'

Me: 'What about Tori? I heard her cussing you out after the game.'

Marcus: 'She'll be alright. After I hit Leslie in the backseat of the whip, I'll buy Tori some shoes or something and she'll take me back.'

Me: 'You think it's that easy?'

Marcus: 'Fool. I'm the man… I know it is."

Brandon looks up from his phone with a smirk. "Leslie, I just thought you should know what his intentions were just in case he tries to pull over in a dark alley or something." My face instantly turns red with embarrassment and the tears pour down my cheeks like rain. Kyra hurries over to me and wraps her arms around my devastated body. I glare at Marcus with heartbroken eyes even though he can't bring himself to face me. I glance at Tori, who is so upset that she's crying as well.

"You are a chauvinistic pig!" Tori screams before rushing through the crowd. Brandon displays a victorious grin before he follows her. The crowd stares at me and I feel so small that I can barely breathe. I begin to hyperventilate on the spot. Kyra drags me away from their prying eyes quickly.

"Come on. Thomas and I will give you a ride home."

'Yeah, I know. I needed to prove a point. I didn't even want her like that and I still pulled her. I thought it would be hard because I used to torture the heck out of her back in the day, but it was surprisingly easy. She's a lot more gullible than I thought.'

'You think it's that easy?'
Marcus: 'Fool. I'm the man... I know it is."

CHAPTER FIFTEEN
I Need You

I ball up in a fetal position underneath my covers, refusing to get up once my alarm goes off for school. I can't show my face at that place today; not after what happened last night.

"Leslie, you up?" My mom asks through my room door.

"Yes, but I think I'm sick. I'm still laying down," I lie. My mom busts in the room like it's an emergency.

"Baby, are you OK? Let me check you for a fever." She quickly places her hand on my forehead, "You don't feel warm. What hurts?"

"Everything," I answer.

Especially my heart.

"Well, you stay in bed, and I'll make you some soup before work. I'll call you throughout the day to check on you." She smiles at me lovingly before kissing my forehead. She hurries out of my room and closes the door.

I sigh when my text alert goes off. It's yet another message from Marcus. I roll my eyes at the sight of his name before tossing my phone to the side.

If I didn't respond the first 20 times, what makes him think I'll respond now?

My phone goes off again and I get annoyed. I pick it after spotting Kyra's name.

"Girl, if you don't talk to Marcus! I don't know how he got my number, but he keeps texting me like a mad man. I know he's the scum of the earth, but I can't have him texting my phone like this. Thomas will get jealous." I read over her message and shake my head.

I really don't have anything to say to Marcus Tate!

Mom brings me soup, crackers, and ginger ale before she leaves for work. I bite a cracker, but I don't touch my soup.

I'm really not that hungry.

I turn on my TV and flip through the channels uninterestedly. I pause at a commercial for *The Mystery Man Series* when my phone begins to ring. The sight of Marcus's name again takes me over the edge. Tears rush from my eyes once the terrible scenes from last night start playing like a movie in my head. I forward him to voicemail after my heart breaks all over again. He calls back a few seconds later.

"What do you want, Marcus!" I scream, letting my emotions flow from my voice like my tears are doing from my eyes. He holds the phone without saying anything. "Bye! I'm hanging up-"

"Please wait! Baby… I need you." I sigh annoyedly.

"I'm sorry Marcus, but I am no longer your baby-"

"My mom--- My mom isn't doing so good." My crying ceases immediately from the troubling news.

"Oh my God, Marcus! I'm so sorry! What happened?"

"She hasn't woken up from the anesthesia and they don't know why." Marcus starts to weep over the phone. My heart instantly aches for him.

"Marcus, where are you?"

"I just came home to shower and change my clothes. I've been at the hospital since last night. I'm heading back up there now."

"I'll go with you if you want. I'm not going to school today."

"Thank you so much, Les! This means a lot to me. I'll be there in ten minutes."

***

I sit in the waiting room, watching with concern as Marcus and his dad talk to the doctor. They nod their heads a couple of times before heading in my direction. Marcus flops down next to me but Principal Tate remains standing. He addresses us both.

"You guys hungry?" We both shake our heads no, "Come on. You must eat something, especially you, son. You haven't eaten since yesterday sometime." Marcus stares at his father but doesn't respond to him. "I'll just go and grab a few sandwiches and some waters. I'll be right back."

Marcus leans back in his seat once his dad walks off. He rests his head against the wall with a close of his eyes. Pain radiates from his demeanor. I grab his hand caringly and stroke it slowly. He opens his eyes to look at me.

"Thank you so much for being here with me. You're the only person that can keep me calm besides my momma." His eyes fill with tears from the mentioning of her. He wipes them quickly with his shirt.

"Of course… I'm here for you," I reply sweetly. He continues to glare at me with sad eyes. I smile at him warmly. He takes a deep breath before turning his body towards mine.

"I know I don't deserve your kindness-" I place my fingers over his lips to stop him from speaking.

"That's not important right now. We need to concentrate on your mom getting better."

"But it is important; It's important to me. My mom would be so disappointed in me if she knew what I did to you." I sigh and let go of his hand. I really don't want to talk about this right now. It's neither the time, nor the place to rehash what happened last night. I don't think my heart can take revisiting one of the worst moments of my life.

"Please, just let me apologize and get my feelings out in the open. I promise, you don't have to say a word if you don't want, and after I finish, we don't have to talk about this ever again. You don't even have to talk to me pass today… even though I'd be completely broken up if you decided to do that." I stare at him seriously while he gazes deeply in my eyes. I can see the most vulnerable part of his soul for the first time since I've known him. My heart reacts favorably to his openness without my permission. He grabs my hands and holds them in his.

"I'm stupid. I'm so stupid… and arrogant, cocky, and self-centered. I'm everything I accused Tori of being. I'm mean and I'm a bully."

He chokes on his words as if they hurt to be said. I can tell he has the urge to look away, but he's determined to stare into my eyes for his entire spiel, "I thought I was the man. My dad is the principal, so I'm never in trouble. I'm good-looking, tall, athletic and the girls love me. My ego is bigger than anyone's I know."

He pauses and swallows the lump forming in his throat. It's apparent that this is a hard thing for him to do. I can tell that he never allows anyone to see the real him. His insecurities surface in his eyes but he never breaks our gaze. "I hide behind my ego. I know that deep down inside, I'm a terrible person. I never had to face myself until I became your science fair partner. No one has ever challenged me to be a better person before you." He pauses again, "Even after everything I purposely put you through, you still gave me a chance. You still opened your home to me, and you opened your heart to me, too. You were nice to me when I didn't deserve it. I've never encountered someone with a heart so pure. I fell head over heels in love with you before I knew what was happening. I was no match for you." I want to blush, but I successfully fight the urge.

He doesn't deserve my smile.

"I knew what I was feeling and I knew that I loved you, but I couldn't look like a punk in front of my teammates. I had the most popular girl in the school on one arm and the most desired on the other, so I had to gloat. I said all that stuff to Brandon to convince myself that I really didn't want to be with you, but I was just lying to myself. The sad part about all of this is I was still going to go about everything the wrong way until I got the news about my mom-" tears start running down his face, but he doesn't wipe them, "And I needed you. I needed you more than I've ever needed anyone in my entire life… and you were there for me. You were everything I needed and more. I don't deserve you; I know I don't, but you are everything to me."

He starts to cry harder, prompting me to wrap my arms around him. I hold him close as he cries loudly without shame. His dad notices his upset son when he approaches us. He places his hand on Marcus's back in a loving way while tears trickle down his face as well. We console Marcus until his mom's doctor appears.

"Mr. Tate?" Both men look up immediately. Marcus stands up and they both hurry towards the doctor. "We have great news; Mrs. Tate has opened her eyes. She seems to be doing fine. She's asking for you two." Mr. Tate and Marcus verbally express their happiness before hugging each other. They dry their eyes as they follow the doctor to Mrs. Tate's room.

Marcus leans back in his seat once his dad walks off. He rests his head against the wall with a close of his eyes. Pain radiates from his demeanor. I grab his hand caringly and stroke it slowly. He opens his eyes to look at me.

CHAPTER SIXTEEN
ON BENDED KNEES

I don't know I'm asleep until a kiss on the lips awakens me. I open my eyes quickly and see Marcus's face in front of mine.

"I'm sorry if that was out of line, but I just couldn't help myself. You looked so beautiful and angelic that I had to kiss you." I sit up and stretch, trying my best to ignore the intimate gesture.

"How's your mom?" I ask, opening my bottle of water and sipping from it. A huge smile appears on Marcus's face.

"She's doing great. She's awake, alert, and she's eating now. My dad is in the room with her." I smile happily at the news.

"Oh my gosh, that's amazing, Marcus! I'm so glad to hear that." I hug him tightly and he does the same. Our embrace eventually comes to an end, but Marcus is still holding me close.

"I know you gave me a second chance and I blew it… and I know I probably messed up any chance I had of us being together, but I was wondering if we could still be friends? I need you, and I'll settle for any way that you'll have me." He stares at me hopefully. I look down as if I'm not sure what to say. I don't think I can ever trust him again.

"I don't know, Marcus."

"Baby, don't you still love me?" He questions in a low tone. He grabs my chin to guide my gaze to his. My heart reacts to the emotional moment again, "Because I still love you." A single tear manages to slide down my cheek. He brushes it away gently.

"What do I have to do to show you that I'm serious about us? I love you baby, and it kills me that you're hurting because of my stupidity. What we had was so perfect and I screwed everything up. I just want a little bit of that perfection again. Please, Les… I need you." Another tear falls, but I don't respond to his proposition. He wipes that one away as well before kissing me softly. I lose myself in his lips, but I find myself quickly. I shove him away from me.

"I'm sorry, but I can't do this. I can't even show my face at school again after everything that's happened." I stand to my feet and he follows suit. He tries to grab me again but I take a step back, "I'm serious, Marcus. We're done. I can never forgive you for what happened." I turn to walk away from him, "I'll find my own way home."

***

I play sick every day, eating so much soup that the sight of it makes me sick to my stomach. I still rather eat soup for the rest of my life than to step foot in that school again, though. My phone rings and Kyra's face pops up. I answer it quickly.

I miss my best friend.

"Hey girl!"
"Hey! How's the fake illness going?" I laugh.
"So far, so good. I'm dying for a burger and fries, though. I'm so tired of soup."
"I'm sure you are. You've been eating soup for what, four days straight now? I'ma start calling you Campbells." I giggle and shake my head.

"Yeah. One more day of faking and it'll be the weekend. I just need to figure out what I'm going to do about next week."

"You know this is crazy, right? You can't just play sick until the school year is over. What about you being valedictorian? What about the science fair convention? You do know you and Marcus's project was chosen to represent the school, right? You must be there." I sigh loudly after she reminds me of what she texted me about on Tuesday. Somehow, Marcus and I won the "best in the school" ribbon for our science fair assignment. Now, we're supposed to represent our school at the convention this Saturday.

"I know it's crazy, but what else am I supposed to do?"

"How about going to school! Forget about what people think! Marcus has been there taking his licks. Tori and Brandon, too."

"But they're used to being in the limelight. I'm new to this. I'm not built for scandal like them."

"Girl," Kyra sighs, "Just know that I love you and I'm here for you... and Marcus… well… he loves you, too." I make a surprised face. Kyra never brings Marcus up in a positive way.

"Wow, that's a first. I don't think you've ever said anything nice about Marcus before." She sighs again.

"You know I hate him, and this is hard for me to say, but I think he's really, really sorry. Every time someone tries to joke about what happened to you, he checks them. He is always speaking highly of you, and he takes the blame for everything that went wrong between you two. He even brings up the 'L' word a lot. Yes girl, Marcus is going around telling the whole school that he's in love with you." I make a shocked face.

Marcus Tate is broadcasting our love? Hmm... it may be real after all.

"Hello? Les, you there?"

"Yeah," I answer, "Just thinking."

"Listen, I think you should just come to school tomorrow. Give it a chance. I'm telling you; it won't be as bad as you think… and remember, I got your back."

***

I stand facing my locker and close my eyes tightly. Everyone keeps staring at me. I'm five seconds away from freaking out.

"Les, breathe girl!" I glance behind me when I hear Kyra's voice. I exhale when I see her friendly face.

"I'm trying," I admit shakily. She takes a step closer to me.

"You're going to have to take it one second at a time. Don't worry about anything besides making it to each class and getting your work done. Try your hardest not to think about anything else."

"How can I when everyone keeps staring at me?"

"Just ignore them, Les." I sigh as if I don't think I can.

"I can try, but I'm going to need your support. What am I supposed to do about the classes that we're not in together? I'm going to have a total meltdown."

"No you won't! You've got this, girl… and if you find yourself in need of a friendly face and I'm not around, just look at Marcus. It's about time that you make up with him, anyway." I look at her weirdly after her random suggestion. She smirks before glancing down the hallway. I follow her eyes and notice Marcus heading towards us.

She looks at me again, "I told Thomas I'll link up with him before first hour. I'll see you later." She rubs my arm before walking away. When she moves past Marcus, they nod their heads at each other.

Was this a setup?

I face my locker again as he closes in on me. I shut my eyes tightly once I realize that I'm not ready for our interaction.

"Hey," he says awkwardly. I take a deep breath. I count to three before turning around to face him.

"Hey," I say back, staring at his handsome face.

I had no idea how much I missed him until now.

"You look amazing baby--- I mean Leslie." He corrects himself.

"You don't look so bad yourself, but I'm sure you already know that," I spit out sarcastically. He looks embarrassed.

"I miss you."

I'm taken aback by how sincere he sounds, but then I immediately realize that he's always sounded sincere. I get angry when I realize that I don't know when he's lying and when he's telling the truth. He stares at me as if he can read my mind, "I'm serious, baby. I do... I really do. I can't eat, I can't sleep… I love you." I stare at him, but I refuse to respond. He steps closer and grabs my waist, "Please, give me another chance, I'm begging you. What do I have to do?"

"How am I supposed to know that you're being honest with me this time? I could have sworn you were telling me the truth before, but you weren't. Why should I believe that you're not trying to play me again?"

He looks down the hall and glances at our classmates. Without warning, he proceeds to get on his knees in front of me. Nervousness covers both of our faces at the same time. Everyone walking past is gawking at us. I feel embarrassed all over again.

"I made a fool out of you, so I'm about to make a fool out of myself and beg for your forgiveness in front of the entire school. As cocky and conceited as I am, I'm still on my knees in this dirty hallway because I love you."

People start pulling out their phones to record us. I cover my face with one hand and he takes the other in his. "Leslie Thompson, I'm a butthole. I manipulated you and broke your heart, and I'm so, so sorry. Please baby, forgive me. I need you. I love you, and I promise, I will never hurt you again."

I finally remove my hand and stare down at him. He looks as embarrassed as I feel. I secretly admire him for being brave enough to expose his vulnerability to the whole school.

It's time for me to be brave, too.

I bend down fearlessly to engage with him. He caresses my cheek as if he and I are the only people around. I grab the sides of his face and kiss him deeply. The whole hallway starts to whistle and cheer. We melt into a kiss that is driven by love. We do so until his dad shows up.

"Excuse me, students! I think first hour has begun!" His deep voice startles us all. We get up from the floor while our classmates scurry to class.

"Sorry, dad. I was just getting my girl back," Marcus says proudly. He wraps his arms around me and I blush. His dad smiles at the good news.

"Well, it's about time. I was getting tired of hearing you crying yourself to sleep every night."

"Ha-ha-ha," Marcus responds sarcastically. We laugh immediately afterwards.

"Just get to class you two." His father pats Marcus's shoulder before walking away. Marcus looks down at me and kisses my lips again.

"Thank you for giving me another chance, baby. I swear, I'm not losing you again."

"I'm sorry, but I can't do this. I can't even show my face at school again after everything that's happened." I stand to my feet and he follows suit. He tries to grab me again but I take a step back, "I'm serious, Marcus. We're done. I can never forgive you for what happened."

CHAPTER SEVENTEEN
THE SCIENCE FAIR CONVENTION

I fix Marcus's button-down shirt and he looks at me nervously. He fixes his collar and takes a deep breath.

"How does this blue shirt look? I look awful, don't I? Man, I knew I should have worn the gray one." He starts rambling, causing me to place my hands on his chest.

"Marcus, calm down. You look fine." I smile at him, and he finally smiles at me. I head over to our project to make sure everything is in order. He blows air forcefully out of his mouth before rubbing his hands together.

"I don't know how you do this every year, baby. This presentation stuff is so nerve-racking!" I look at him and shake my head.

"I can say the same thing about you, Mr. Football Star. How do you do that every year?" He pauses and thinks about my words.

"I don't know. I guess you have a point. I just go out there and do what I love." I look at him with a grin.

"Exactly." He grins back. I tackle a few finishing touches with Marcus's help. He grabs me around the waist once we finish.

"You are so freaking smart and amazing." His compliments always make me blush.

"You're pretty darn smart yourself. You're standing on this stage with me this year instead of Kyra. That's a big deal." He looks at me sideways.

"Girl, please. We both know the truth. You used your good idea for our project and then did most of the work yourself. This is literally all you." We both chuckle, "Thank you, though. I never thought I'd be competing in the science fair convention. My mom and dad are over the moon about this. They already want me to marry you." I giggle at his words and hit him playfully on the arm.

"Hey, Team Cooley High, you're going on next," the backstage worker of the convention says. I look at Marcus and cheese excitedly.

"Oh my gosh, this is it!" I exclaim in a giddy tone while Marcus looks like he's ready to puke. I grab his face and stare into his eyes, "Hey babe, this is our championship game; me and you against these other teams. We've got this." He places his forehead on mine and smiles devilishly.

"Did you say our championship game? Then hecky yeah... we definitely got this!"

***

Marcus and I walk into the ballroom with the first-place trophy in hand. Everyone that came out to support us cheers as soon as they see us.

"Hey, congratulations!"

"Marcus and Leslie, congratulations!"

"Ok, y'all! I see y'all! Relationship goals! Congratulations!"

Marcus and I walk through a sea of praises until Kyra steps in our way. She looks at us seriously for a moment, but then smiles from ear to ear.

"Y'all were the bomb up there; way to kick butt." She hugs me and I thank her, "And you... Marcus Tate... even though you stole my spot and my best friend, you looked good up there with her. Congratulations." They smile at each other and Kyra hugs him as well. Thomas walks up behind her and shakes his head.

"Hey, man. Unhand my girl!" Marcus and Thomas laugh as they reach in for a bro hug. "Congratulations, man. That was pretty dope. It's good to see you displaying your talents on a different stage."

"Thanks bro, I appreciate it."

We talk to them for another minute or two until we spot our parents. We are surprised to see my mom with his dad. We walk up to them both.

"Hey mom… Principal Tate."

"Sup dad and Ms. Thompson." Both of our parents smile proudly at us.

"Hello, first place winners! I'm so proud of you two." We both give Principal Tate our thanks. He looks in my direction, "I came over to talk to your mom about how amazing of a student you are and how excellent you've been to my son. I see her at the convention every year, but I never get a chance to talk with her." My mom appears flattered before addressing me as well.

"Baby, you did it! Four years in a row… congratulations!" My mom hugs me and Marcus's dad chimes in.

"Which is a school record, by the way." I smile even harder.

"And congratulations to you, too, young man. I'm so proud of you both." He grins at my mom and thanks her as well.

"Son, I knew you had it in you." Marcus holds up the trophy while flashing his perfect smile. "I know it really bothered you that you didn't win the championship football game-" Marcus stops his father in mid-sentence.

"You're right, dad. It sucked to go undefeated just to get beat in the end, but this right here is my real championship trophy." He stares at it for a second before looking at me, "And it's all because of this woman right here. I've finally found the perfect teammate." He wraps his arms around me and I blush.

"Thanks, babe. You're not too bad yourself." Everyone laughs as I look up at him. "I guess we do make a pretty good science fair pair."

www.ingramcontent.com/pod-product-compliance
Lightning Source LLC
Chambersburg PA
CBHW071158300726
48975CB00004B/1209